T0165858

The Grain Ship

The Grain Ship
Morgan Robertson

MINT EDITIONS

The Grain Ship was first published in 1914.

This edition published by Mint Editions 2021.

ISBN 9781513281490 | E-ISBN 9781513286518

Published by Mint Editions®

 MINT
EDITIONS

minteditionbooks.com

Publishing Director: Jennifer Newens
Design & Production: Rachel Lopez Metzger
Project Manager: Micaela Clark
Typesetting: Westchester Publishing Services

Contents

THE GRAIN SHIP

I could not help listening to the talk at the next table, because the orchestra was quiet and the conversation unrestrained; then, too, a nautical phrasing caught my ear and aroused my attention. For I had been a lifelong student of nautical matters. A side glance showed me the speaker, a white-haired, sunburned old fellow in immaculate evening dress. With him at the table in the restaurant were other similarly clad men, evidently of good station in life, and in their answers and comments these men addressed the white-haired man as Commodore. A navy captain, I thought, promoted on retirement. His talk bore it out.

"Yes, sirree," he said, as he thumped the table mildly. "A good, tight merchant ship, with nothing wrong except what might be ascribed to neglect such as light canvas blown away and ropes cast off the pins, with no signs of fire, leak, or conflict to drive the crew out, with plenty of grub in the stores and plenty of water in the tanks. Yet, there she was, under topsails and topgallant-sails, rolling along before a Biscay sea, and deserted, except that the deck was almost covered with dead rats."

"What killed them, Commodore," asked one; "and what happened to the crew?"

"Nobody knows. It might have been a poisonous gas from the cargo, but if so it didn't affect us after we boarded her. The log-book was gone, so we got no information from that. Moreover, every boat was in its chocks or under its own davits. It was as though some mysterious power had come down from above and wiped out the crew, besides killing the rats in the hold. She was a grain ship from 'Frisco, and grain ships are full of rats.

"I was the prize-lieutenant that took her into Queenstown. She was condemned in Admiralty proceedings and, later, restored to her owners. But to this day no man has told the story of that voyage. It is thirty years and more since then, but it will remain one of the unexplained mysteries of the sea."

The party left the table a little later, and left me, an ex-sailor, in a condition of mind not due to the story I had heard from the Commodore. There was something else roused into activity—something indefinite, intangible, elusive, like the sense of recognition that comes to you when you view a new scene that you know you have never seen before. It was nothing pertaining to myself or my adventures; and I had never heard of a ship being found deserted with all boats in place. It was something I must have heard at some time and place that bore no relation to the sea and its mysteries. It tormented me; I worried myself into insomnia that night, thinking about it, but at last fell asleep, and awakened in the morning with a memory twenty-five years old.

It is a long stretch of time and space from that gilded restaurant of that night to the arid plans of Arizona, and back through the years of work and struggle and development to the condition of a sailor on shore beating his way, horseback and afoot, across the country from the Gulf to the Pacific. But in my sleep I traversed it, and, lying on my back in the morning, puffing at my first pipe, I lived again my experience with the half-witted tramp whom I had entertained in my camp and who changed his soul in my presence.

I was a line-rider for a cattle company, and as it was before the days of wire fences, my work was to ride out each day along my boundary and separate the company's cattle from those of its neighbor, a rival company. It was near the end of the day, when I was almost back to camp, that I saw him coming along the road, with the peculiar swing to his shoulders and arms that, once acquired, never leaves the deep-water sailor; so I had no hesitancy in greeting him after the manner of seamen.

"Well, mate, how are you heading?" I inquired, as I leaned over the saddle.

"Say, pardner," he said, in a soft, whining voice, "kin you tell me where a feller might git a bite to eat around here?"

"Well," I answered, "yes and no. I thought you were a sailorman." Only his seamanly roll had appealed to me. His face, though bearded, tanned, and of strong, hard lines, seemed weak and crafty. He was tall, and strongly built—the kind of man who impresses you at first sight as accustomed to sudden effort of mind and body; yet he cringed under my stare, even as I added, "Yes, I'll feed you." I had noticed a blue foul anchor tattooed on his wrist.

"Come along, old man," I said, kindly. "You're traveling for your health. I'll ask no fool questions and say nothing about you. My camp is just around that hill."

He walked beside my horse, and we soon reached the camp, a log house of one room, with an adobe fireplace and chimney, a rough table, and a couple of boxes for seats. Also, there was a plank floor, a novelty and a luxury in that country at that time. Under this floor was a family of huge rats that I had been unable to exterminate, and I had found it easier and cheaper to feed them than to have them gnawing into my stores in my absence. So they had become quite tame, and in the evenings, keeping at a safe distance, however, they would visit me. I had no fear of them, and rather enjoyed their company.

I fed and hobbled my horse, then cooked our supper, of which my guest ate voraciously. After supper I filled my pipe and offered him another, but he refused it; he did not smoke. Then I talked with him and found him weak-minded. He knew nothing of consequence, nothing of the sea or of sailors, and he had forgotten when that anchor had been tattooed on his wrist. He thought it had always been there. He was a laborer, a pick-and-shovel man, and this was the only work he aspired to. Disappointed in him, for I had yearned for a little seamanly sympathy and companionship, I finished my smoke in the fire-light and turned to get the bed ready, when one of the rats sprang from the bed, across the floor and between the tramp and the fire; then it darted to a hole in the edge of the floor and disappeared. But its coming and going wrought a curious effect upon that wayfarer. He choked, spluttered, stood up and reeled, then fell headlong to the floor.

"Hello!" I said, anxiously; "anything wrong?"

He got on his feet, looked wildly about the place, and asked, in a hoarse, broken voice that held nothing of its former plaintiveness:

"What's this? Was I picked up? What ship is this?"

"No ship at all. It's a cow camp."

"Log cabin, isn't it?"—he was staring at the walls. "I never saw one before. I must have been out of my head for a while. Picked up, of course. Was the mate picked up? He was in bad shape."

"Look here, old man," I said, gently, "are you out of your head now, or were you out of your head before?"

"I don't know. I must have been out of my head. I can't remember much after tumbling overboard, until just now. What day is this?"

"Tuesday," I answered.

"Tuesday? It was Sunday when it happened. Did you have a hand in picking me up? Who was it?"

"Not me," I said. "I found you on the road out here in a dazed state of mind, and you knew nothing whatever of ships or of sailors, though I took you for a shellback by your walk."

"That's right. You can always spot one. You're a sailor, I can see, and an American, too. But what are you doing here? This must be the coast of Portugal or Spain."

"No, this is a cow camp on the Crossbar Range in the middle of Arizona."

"Arizona? Six thousand miles from there! How long have I been out of my head?"

"Don't know. I've only known you since sundown. You've just gone through a remarkable change of front."

"What day of the month is it?"

"The third day of December."

"Hell! Six months ago. It happened in June, Of course, six months is time enough for me to get here, but why can't I remember coming? Someone must have brought me."

"Not necessarily. You were walking along, caring for yourself, but hungry. I brought you here for a feed and a night's sleep."

"That was kind of you—" He involuntarily raised his hand to his face. "I've grown a beard, I see. Let's see how I look with a beard." He stepped to a looking-glass on the wall, took one look, and sprang back.

"Why, it isn't me!" he exclaimed, looking around with dilated eyes. "It's someone else."

"Take another look," I said. He did so, moved his head to the right and left, and then turned to me.

"It must be me," he said, hoarsely, "for the image in the glass follows my movements. But I've lost my face. I'm another man. I don't know myself."

"Look at that anchor on your wrist," I suggested. He did so.

"Yes," he said, "that part of me is left. It was pricked in on my first voyage." He examined his arms and legs. "Changed," he muttered. He rubbed his knees, and passed his hands over his body.

"What year was it when, as you say, you jumped overboard?" I asked.

"Eighteen seventy-five."

"This is eighteen eighty-four. Matey, you have been nine years out of your head," I said.

"Nine years? Sure? Can you prove that to me? My God, man, think of it! Nine years gone out of my life. You don't know what that means to me."

I showed him a faded and discolored newspaper.

"That paper is about six months old," I said, "but it's an eighteen eighty-four paper."

"Right," he said, sadly and somewhat wildly. "Got a pipe? I want to smoke on this, and think it out. Nine years, and six thousand miles travel!

MORGAN ROBERTSON

Where have I been, I wonder, and what have I done, to change the very face of me, while I lived with it? It's something like death, I take it."

I gave him a pipe and tobacco, and he smoked vigorously, trembling with excess of emotion, yet slowly pulling himself together. Finally he steadied, but he could not smoke. He put the pipe down, saying that it sickened him. I knew nothing of psychology at the time, but think now that in his second personality he had given up smoking.

I forbore questioning him, knowing that I could not help him in his problem—that he must work it out himself. He did not sleep that night, and kept me awake most of the time with his twitchings and turnings. Once he was up, examining his face in the glass by the light of a match, but in the morning, after a doze of an hour or so, I found him outside, looking at the sunrise and smoking.

"I'm getting used to my new face," he said, "and I'm getting used to smoking again. Got to. Nothing but a smoke will help a fellow at times. What business is this you're in here?"

"Cow-punching—riding out after cattle."

"Hard to learn?"

"Easy for a sailor. I'm only hanging on until pay-day, then I make for 'Frisco to ship."

"And someone will take your place, I suppose. I'll work for my grub if you'll break me in so that I can get the job. I'm through with going to sea."

"Certainly. All I need is to tell the boss. I've an extra saddle."

So I tutored him in the tricks of cow-punching, and found him an apt pupil. But he was heavy and depressed, seeming to be burdened with some terrible experience, or memory, that he was trying to shake off. It was not until the evening before my departure, when I had secured him the job and we sat smoking before the mesquite-root fire, that he took me into his confidence. The friendly rat had again appeared, and he sprang up, backed away, and sat down again, trembling violently.

"It was that rat that brought you to yourself that evening," I ventured. "Rats must have had something to do with your past life."

"Right, they did," he answered, puffing fiercely. "I didn't know you had rats here, though."

"A whole herd of them under the floor. But they're harmless. I found them good company."

"I found them bad company. I was shipmates with thousands of rats on that last passage. Want the yarn? It'll raise your hair."

I was willing, and he reeled it off. His strong self-control never left him from the beginning to the end, though the effect upon me was not only to raise my hair, but at times to stop the beating of my heart. I left him next morning, and have never seen or heard of him since; but there is strong reason to believe that he never went to sea again, or told that yarn in shipping circles. And it is because I have not seen that old Commodore since the evening in the restaurant, and because I cannot recall the name of the ship, or secure full data of marine happenings of the year 1875, that I am giving that story to the world in this form, hoping it will reach the right quarters and explain to those interested the mystery of the grain ship, found in good shape, but abandoned by all but the dead rats.

"I SHIPPED IN HER AT 'Frisco," began Draper. "She was a big, skysail-yarder loading grain at Oakland, and as the skipper had offered me second mate's berth, I went over and sized her up. She seemed all right, as far as man may judge of a ship in port—nearly new, and well found in gear and canvas, which the riggers had rove off and bent. Her cargo of grain was nearly in, and there would be nothing much to do in the way of hard work. Still, I couldn't make up my mind. Something seemed to prevent me liking the prospect, so I went on up to Oakland to visit some friends, and on the way back, long after dark, stopped again at the dock for another look at her. And this time I saw what was needed to ease my mind and decide me. You know as well as I do that rats quit a ship bound for the bottom, and their judgment is always right, though no one knows why. And I reasoned that if rats swarm into an outbound ship she would have a safe passage. Well, that's what they were doing. Wharf rats, a foot long—hundreds of them—going up the mooring-chains, the cable to the dock, the lines, the fenders, and the gangway, some over the rail, others in through the mooring-chocks. The watchman was quiet, perhaps asleep; so, perhaps, every rat that went aboard got into the hold. I signed on next morning.

"Nothing occurred aboard that ship except the usual trouble of breaking in a new crew, until we'd got down to about forty south, when the skipper brought up a rat-trap with a big, healthy rat in it. He was a mild-mannered little man, and a rat and dog fight marked the limits of his sporting nature. That was what he was after. He had a little black-and-tan terrier, about the size of the rat, and there was a lively time around the deck for a while, until the rat got away. He put up a stiff

MORGAN ROBERTSON

fight with the dog, but finally saw his chance, and slipped into the forward companion of the cabin; then, I suppose, he found the hole he'd come up. But the dog had nipped him once, it seemed, for the rat left a tiny trail of blood after him. As for the dog, he nearly had a fit in his anger and disappointment, and when the skipper picked him up he nipped him, too. It was only a little wound on the skipper's thumb, but the dog's teeth were sharp, and the blood had come. The skipper gave him a licking, and the work went on.

"The dog was a spirited little fellow, and used to sit on the skipper's shoulder when we were going about, or wearing ship, or handling canvas, and he would bark and yelp and swear at us, bossing each job as though he knew all about it. It kept the men good-humored, and we all liked the little beast. But from the time of the licking he moped, and finally grew sick, slinking around the deck in a dispirited fashion, refusing any attention, and unwilling to remain a minute in one place. We felt rather sore at the skipper, who seemed ashamed now and anxious to make friends with the dog, for the little bite in his thumb had healed up. This went on for a few days, and then we woke up to what really ailed that dog. He was racing around decks one morning with his tongue hanging out, froth dropping from his mouth, and agonized yelps and whines coming from him.

"'My God!' cried the skipper, 'Now I know. He was bitten in 'Frisco. He is mad, and he has bitten me. Keep away from him everybody. Don't let him get near you.'

"I'll always count that in the skipper's favor. Bitten and doomed himself, he thought of others.

"We dodged the little brute until he had dropped in sheer exhaustion and gone into a spasm. Then we picked him up with a couple of shovels and threw him overboard. But this didn't end it, for the skipper was bitten. He studied up some books on medicine he had below, but found no comfort. I heard him tell the mate that there was nothing in the medicine chest to meet such an emergency.

"'In fact,' he said, mournfully, 'even on shore, with the best of medical skill, there is no hope for a man bitten by a mad dog. The period of incubation is from ten days to a year. I will navigate the ship until I lose my head, Mr. Barnes; then, for fear of harm to yourselves, you must shoot me dead. I am doomed, anyway.'

"We tried to reassure him, but his mind was made up and nothing would change it. Whether or not he had hydrophobia we could not tell at the time, but we knew that strong and intense thinking about it would bring on symptoms. In the light of after happenings, however, there was no doubt of it. He got sick after we'd rounded the Horn, fidgety, nervous, and excitable, and, like the dog, he couldn't stay long in one place; but he wouldn't admit that the disease had developed in him until the little scar on his thumb grew inflamed and painful and he experienced difficulty in drinking. Then he gave up, but he certainly showed courage and character.

"'I am against suicide on principle,' he said to Mr. Barnes and me, 'so I must not kill myself. But I am not against killing a wild beast that menaces the lives of human beings. I am to be such a wild beast. Kill me in time before I injure you.'

"But we didn't. We had the same compunctions about killing a sick man that he had about suicide. We strapped him down when he got violent, and after three days of frightful physical and mental agony he died. We buried him with the usual ceremonies, and Mr. Barnes took command.

"He and I had a consultation. We were well up toward the river Plate, and he was for putting into Montevideo and cabling the owners for orders. As he was a competent navigator I advised keeping on; and in this, perhaps, is where I earned my punishment. He took my advice, and we had reached up into the doldrums on the line, when a man turned out at eight bells of the middle watch—midnight, you know— and swore that a big rat had bitten him as he lay asleep. We laughed at him, even though he showed four bloody little holes in his wrist. But, three weeks later, that man was raving around the deck, going into periodic convulsions, frothing at the mouth, and showing every symptom that had preceded the death of the skipper. He died in the same horrible agony, and we realized that not only the skipper, but the rat bitten by the dog had been inoculated with the virus, and that the rat could inoculate other rats. We buried the man, and from that time on slept in our boots, with mittens on, and our heads covered, even in the hot weather of the tropics. It was no use. Mad rats appeared on deck, frenzied with pain, frothing at the mouth, fearless of all living things, a few at first and after dark, then in larger numbers night and day. We killed them as we could, but they increased. They filled the cabin and forecastles, and we found them in coils of rope up aloft in the tops, the crosstrees, and the doublings of the masts. They climbed everywhere, up or down, on a sail or its leach, a single rope or a backstay. The mate and myself, with the steward, could shut the doors of our rooms and keep them out until they chose to gnaw through, but the poor devils forward had no such refuge. Their forecastles and the galley and carpenter shop were wide open. Man after man was nipped, awake or asleep, on deck or below, or up aloft in the dark, when, reaching for another hold on a shroud or a backstay, he would touch something soft and furry, and feel the teeth and hear the squeak that spelled death for him.

"In two weeks from the death of the first sailor, seven others were sick; and all went through the symptoms—restlessness, talkativeness, and the tendency to belittle the case and to deny their danger. But the real symptom, which they had to accept themselves, was their inability to drink water. It was frightful to see the poor wretches, staggering around with eyes wide open and the terrible fear of death in them, going to the barrel for a drink, only to tumble back in convulsions at the sight of the water. We strapped them down as they needed it, and they died, one by one; for there was no helping them.

"We had started with a crew of twenty, a carpenter, sailmaker, steward, and cook, besides the mate and myself. Eight were gone now, and from the exhaustion of the remainder, due to extra work and loss of sleep, it became difficult to work ship. Men aloft moved slowly, fearing at any moment the sting of small, sharp teeth. Skysails, royals, and staysails blew away before men could get up to furl them. Gear that had parted was left unrove; for a panic-stricken crew cannot be bullied or coerced. Any of them would take a knock-down from the mate or myself rather than go aloft at night.

"We got clear of the doldrums in time, and by then six more of the crew, including the cook, had been bitten, and things looked bad. I now strongly advised the mate to put in to St.-Louis or some other port on the African coast, land the crew, and wait until the last rat had been bitten by his fellow and died; but he would not have it. To land the men, he said, meant to lose them, and to wait until another crew was sent by the owners. This would be loss of time, money, and prospects. I could only give way, even though the last item pertained solely to him. I was not a navigator, and did not hope for promotion to a command.

"So we held on, dodging the crazed men when the disease had reached their brains, knocking them down and binding them when necessary, and watching them die in their tracks like so many mad dogs. And all this time the number of rats that sought the deck for light and air was increasing. We carried belaying pins in our boots now, ready to swipe a rat that got too close; but as for killing them all this way, it was beyond any chance. There were too many, and they ran too fast. Before the six men had died, others had been bitten, and one had felt the teeth of a maddened shipmate. So the terrible game continued; we had only seven men before the mast now, and the carpenter and sailmaker had to drop their work and stand watch, while the steward quit being a steward to cook for those that were left.

"The man at the wheel had heard me arguing with the mate about making port, and, counting upon my sympathy, had prevailed upon the others forward to insist upon it. Well, you know the feeling of an officer up against mutiny. No matter what the provocation, he must put the mutiny down; so, when the men came aft, they found me with the mate, and dead against them. We called their bluff, drove them forward at the muzzles of our guns, and promised them relief from all work except handling sail if they would take the ship to Queenstown. They agreed, because they could not do anything else, and the mutiny was over. But my conscience bothered me later on; for if I had joined them, some lives might have been saved. Even though the mate was a big, courageous Irish-American half again as heavy as myself, he could not have held out against me with the crew at my back. But, you see, it would have been mutiny, and mutiny spells with a big M to a man that knows the law.

"Before we reached the Bay of Biscay every man forward, including the carpenter, sailmaker, and steward, had been bitten, either by a mad rat or a mad shipmate, and was more or less along on the way to convulsions and death. The decks, rails, and rigging, the tops, crosstrees, and yards, swarmed with rats darting along aimlessly biting each other, and going on, frothing at their little mouths, and squeaking in pain. By this time all thought of handling the ship was gone from us. The mate and I took turns at steering, and keeping our eyes open for a sail. But a curious thing about that passage is that from the time we dropped the Farallones, off 'Frisco, we did not speak a single craft in all that long four months of sailing. Once in a while a steamer's smoke would show up on the horizon, and again a speck that might be a sail would heave in sight for an hour or so; but nothing came near us.

"The mate and I began to quarrel. We had heeled ourselves with pistols against a possible assault of some frenzied sailor, but there was strong chance that we might use these playthings on each other. I upbraided the mate for not putting in to St.-Louis, and he got back at me for advising him against putting in to Montevideo. It was not

MORGAN ROBERTSON

an even argument, for the first sailor had not been bitten at the time I advised him. But it resulted in bad feeling between us. We kept our tempers, however, and kept the maddened men away from us until they died, one by one; then, with the wheel in beckets, and the ship steering herself before the wind, we hove the bodies overboard. There was no funeral service now; we had become savages.

"'Well,' said the mate, as the last body floated astern, 'that's done. Take your wheel. I'm going to sleep.'

"'Look out,' I said, grimly, 'that it's not your last.'

"'What do you mean?' he asked, eying me in an ugly way. 'Do you strike sleeping men?'

"'No; but rats bite sleeping men,' I answered. 'And understand, Mr. Barnes, I'd rather you'd live than die, so that I may live myself. With both alive and one awake a passing ship could be seen and signaled. With one dead and the other asleep, a ship might pass by. I shall keep a lookout.'

"'Oh, that's all, is it? Well, if that's all, keep your lookout.' His ugly disposition still held him. He went down, and I steered, keeping a sharp lookout around; for I knew that up in the bay there were sure chances of something coming along. But nothing appeared, and before an hour had passed, Mr. Barnes was up, sucking his wrist, and looking wildly at me.

"'My God, Draper,' he said, 'I've got it! I killed the rat, but he's killed me.'

"'Well, Mr. Barnes,' I said, as he strode up to me, 'I'm sorry for you; but what do you want?—what I would want in your place?—a bullet through the head?'

"'No, no.' He sucked madly at his wrist, where showed the four little red spots.

"'Well, I'll tell you, Barnes. You've shown antagonism to me, and you're likely to carry it into your delirium when it comes. I'll not shoot you until you menace me; then, unless I am too far gone myself, I'll shoot you dead, not only in self-defense, but as an act of mercy.'

"'And you?' he rejoined. 'You—you—you are to live and get command of the ship?'

"'No,' I answered, hotly. 'I can't get command. I'm not certificated. I want my life, that's all.'

"He left me without another word, and stamped forward. Rats ran up his clothing, reaching for his throat, but he brushed them off and went on, around the forward house, and then aft to me.

"'Draper,' he said, in a choked voice, 'I've got to die. I know it. I know it as none of the men knew it. And it means more to me.'

"'No, it doesn't. Life was as sweet to them as to you or the skipper.'

"'But I've a Master's license. All I wanted was my chance, and I thought my chance had come. Draper, if I'd taken this ship into port I'd have been a hero and obtained my command.'

"'So, that's your cheap way of looking at it, is it?' I answered, as I hove on the wheel and kicked rats from underfoot. 'A hero by the toll of twenty-four deaths. Down off the river Plate I didn't realize the horror of all this. Off St.-Louis I did, and advised you. You withstood, to be a hero. Well, I'm sorry for you, that's all.'

"A big rat jumped from the wheel-box at this moment, climbed my clothing, and had reached my chest before I knocked it off with my fist.

"'You see, Barnes, the rat does not know, and I did not kill it. But you do know, and I shall hasten your death with a bullet if you approach me. It will not be murder, nor manslaughter. It will be an act of mercy; but I cannot do it now. See how I feel?'

"'Oh, God!' he shrieked, running away from me. He reached the break of the poop, then turned and came back.

"'Got your gun on you, Draper? Kill me now; kill me, and have it over with. I'm down and done for. There's nothing more for me.'

"I refused; and yet I know that with regard to that man's mental agony for the next few days, culminating in the first physical symptoms of unrest, fever, and thirst, I should have obeyed his request. He was doomed, and knew it. And he was a madman from mental causes before the physical had produced effects, even though the disease ran its course quickly in him. On the third day he was raving of a black-eyed woman who kept a candy store in Boston, and who had promised to marry him when he obtained command.

"I got out a bottle of bromide from the medicine chest and induced Barnes to take a good dose of it. He drank about half a teacup of it, and in an hour was asleep. Then, clad in boots and mittens, with a sailor's clothes-bag over my head, I went aloft and lashed myself in the mizzentopmast crosstrees, where I obtained about six hours' sleep, which I needed badly. Barnes was worse when I came down; three more rats had bitten him, he declared, and he begged me to shoot him. It never occurred to him to do the job himself, and I couldn't suggest it to him.

"'Well, Draper,' he said at last, 'I'm going, and I know it. Now, if you escape, sometime you'll be in Boston. Will you take the street-car out the Boston Road, and at Number 24 Middlesex Place drop in and say a few words to that woman? Call her Kate, and say we were shipmates, and I told you to. Tell her about this, and that I thought of her, and didn't want to die because of her. Tell her, will you, Draper?'

"'Barnes, I promise,' I said. 'I will hunt up or write to that woman if I get ashore. I'll tell her all about it. Now, go and lie down.'

"But he couldn't lie down; and when the time came that I had to sleep in the crosstrees again, I found, on waking, that Barnes had followed me, and in some way had got my gun out of my pocket. I knew he had it by the insane way he laughed as I came down from my perch. I hunted through the cabin for pistols or rifles, but he had been ahead of me; and as I came up and he stood near the wheel—the wheel, like everything else, was neglected now—there was a crazy look in his eyes that meant bad luck for me.

"'Going to kill me, weren't you?' he chuckled. 'Well, you won't. Nor will you get that woman out the Boston Road. I'm dead on to you, you dog. And you'll get no credit for the advice you gave—that I put down in the log. Not much you won't.'

"He darted into the cabin and returned with the ship's log, which he had charge of, and the official log of the skipper. I do not know what was entered in them, but he tossed them overboard.

"'There goes your record of efficiency,' he said.

"He came toward me on the run, his eyes blazing, but I did not budge. He made no gun-play, but put up his fists, and I met him; I was used to this form of fighting. However, I went down before his plunges and punches, and realized that I was up against a bigger, heavier, stronger man than myself, and could not hope to win. I'm no small boy, as you see, but Barnes was a giant, and a skilled fighter.

"I got away from him and kept away. I wanted to hoist an ensign, union down, but the lunatic prevented me; his intelligence had left him. He watched me as a cat watches a mouse, or I might have brought a handspike down on his head and ended his troubles and some of my own. And it would have been no foul play to have done so; but I could not. He followed me everywhere, ready to pounce upon me at the first move I made.

"I spent that night walking away from him as he nosed me around the deck, and brushing off the crazy rats that climbed my legs. I did not dare make for the rigging, for without my bag I would have been worse off than on deck, and at such a move he would have jumped on me.

But in the morning he had his first convulsion, and it left him a wreck. While he lay gasping and choking on the deck, with equally afflicted rats crawling over him and nipping where they felt flesh, I managed to get a bite from the steward's storeroom, and it roused me up and strengthened me. I came out, resolved to bind him down, but I was too late. He was on his feet, the paroxysm gone, crazy as ever, and, though weak, still able to master me.

"The ship was rolling heavily in the trough of a Biscay sea, which, no matter how the wind, is a violent, troublesome heave of cross-forces. The upper canvas was carried away, or hanging in the buntlines. Some of the braces were adrift and the yards swinging. We had the courses clewed up when the men were alive, and the lower yards were fairly square; so the ship, with the aid of the head-sails, kept the canvas full, and she sailed along, manned by a crew of rabid rats, a crazy first mate, and a half-crazy second mate. I knew I was half-crazy, for I had a fixed, insistent thought that would not go—that of a little school-ma'am who had whipped me in childhood. I deserved the whipping, but—Lord, how I hated her now!

"I feared the mate. He was again nosing me around the deck, glaring murder at me and talking to himself. I feared him more than I feared the rats, for I could brush them off. I could not get out of his sight; but I did venture on grabbing a circular life-buoy from the quarter-rail as I passed it, and slipping it over my head, and he did not seem to notice the maneuver. I was resolved, as a last resort, to jump into the sea with this scant protection against death by drowning, hunger, or thirst, rather than risk another assault by this lunatic or a bite from a rat. These were numbered now by the thousands. The deck was black with them in places, and here and there a rope was as big around as a stove-pipe.

"All was quiet this last day aboard. The mate busied himself in following me around, talking to the rats and to himself, even as they bit him, and I busied myself in quietly keeping out of his way and brushing off rats that climbed my legs. I was dead tired, being on my feet so long, and in sheer desperation and love of life I hoped for another convulsion that would give me relief from the strain. But before it came to him I was out of his way, and, I strongly suspect, he was out of the way of the convulsion.

"He caught me on the forecastle deck and made for me, half mad from the disease, but wholly mad from his mental state. There was no escape except out the head-gear, and I went that way, with him after me. Out the bowsprit, on to the jib foot-ropes, and out toward the end

I went, hoping to reach the martingale-stay and slip down it to the back-ropes. I did so, but he scrambled down, tumbling and clutching, and gripped me just abaft the dolphin-striker. His face was twisted in frenzy, and he growled and barked like a dog, occasionally breaking into a horrible, rat-like squeal. But he didn't bite me; he simply squeezed me in both arms, and in that effort lost his hold on the back-rope and fell, taking me with him. We struck the water together, and his grip loosened, for he was now up against something too strong for him—the sound and sight and feeling of cold water. When we came up, the cutwater was between us, and I didn't see him again, though I heard his convulsive gurgling and screaming from the other side of the ship. Then the sounds stopped, and I think he must have gone under; but I was too busy with myself to speculate much. I was trying to get a finger-nail grip on that smooth, black side slipping by me, but could not. There was nothing to get hold of, and no ropes were hanging over. Then I thought of the rudder and the iron bumpkin on it that the rudder-chains fastened to, and swam with all my strength under the quarter as it came along. But it was no good. The life-buoy hampered me in swimming, and I missed the rudder by an inch.

"The ship went on and left me alone on the sea. I remember very little of it. I think my mind must have slowly gone out of me, leaving me another person. I remember a few sensations—and it only seems like a week ago to me—one, of being alone on the surface of the sea at night, supported by the life-buoy; and then, I seemed to be back among the rats, but that was just as I wakened on your floor here. The next sensation was the sight of you, and the sound of your voice, speaking to me, and then the knowledge that I was really alive and ashore."

"And the woman out the Boston Road?" I inquired at length.

"I will write to her as I promised. But I will not go there. Boston is too close to the sea."

From the Darkness and the Depths

I had known him for a painter of renown—a master of his art, whose pictures, which sold for high prices, adorned museums, the parlors of the rich, and, when on exhibition, were hung low and conspicuous. Also, I knew him for an expert photographer—an "art photographer," as they say, one who dealt with this branch of industry as a fad, an amusement, and who produced pictures that in composition, lights, and shades rivaled his productions with the brush.

His cameras were the best that the market could supply, yet he was able, from his knowledge of optics and chemistry, to improve them for his own uses far beyond the ability of the makers. His studio was filled with examples of his work, and his mind was stocked with information and opinions on all subjects ranging from international policies to the servant-girl problem.

He was a man of the world, gentlemanly and successful, about sixty years old, kindly and gracious of manner, and out of this kindliness and graciousness had granted me the compliment of his friendship, and access to his studio whenever I felt like calling upon him.

Yet it never occurred to me that the wonderful and technically correct marines hanging on his walls were due to anything but the artist's conscientious study of his subject, and only his casual mispronounciation of the word "leeward," which landsmen pronounce as spelled, but which rolls off the tongue of a sailor, be he former dock rat or naval officer, as "looward," and his giving the long sounds to the vowels of the words "patent" and "tackle," that induced me to ask if he had ever been to sea.

"Why, yes," he answered. "Until I was thirty I had no higher ambition than to become a skipper of some craft; but I never achieved it. The best I did was to sign first mate for one voyage—and that one was my last. It was on that voyage that I learned something of the mysterious properties of light, and it made me a photographer, then an artist. You are wrong when you say that a searchlight cannot penetrate fog."

"But it has been tried," I remonstrated.

"With ordinary light. Yes, of course, subject to refraction, reflection, and absorption by the millions of minute globules of water it encounters."

We had been discussing the wreck of the *Titanic*, the most terrible marine disaster of history, the blunders of construction and management, and the later proposed improvements as to the lowering of boats and the location of ice in a fog.

Among these considerations was also the plan of carrying a powerful searchlight whose beam would illumine the path of a twenty-knot liner and render objects visible in time to avoid them. In regard to this I had contended that a searchlight could not penetrate fog, and if it could, would do as much harm as good by blinding and confusing the watch officers and lookouts on other craft.

"But what other kind of light can be used?" I asked, in answer to his mention of ordinary light.

"Invisible light," he answered. "I do not mean the Röntgen ray, nor the emanation from radium, both of which are invisible, but neither of which is light, in that neither can be reflected nor refracted. Both will penetrate many different kinds of matter, but it needs reflection or refraction to make visible an object on which it impinges. Understand?"

"Hardly," I answered dubiously. "What kind of visible light is there, if not radium or the Röntgen ray? You can photograph with either, can't you?"

"Yes, but to see what you have photographed you must develop the film. And there is no time for that aboard a fast steamer running through the ice and the fog. No, it is mere theory, but I have an idea that the ultraviolet light—the actinic rays beyond the violet end of the spectrum, you know—will penetrate fog to a great distance, and in spite of its higher refractive power, which would distort and magnify an object, it is better than nothing."

"But what makes you think that it will penetrate fog?" I queried. "And if it is invisible itself, how will it illumine an object?"

"As to your first question," he answered, with a smile, "it is well known to surgeons that ultraviolet light will penetrate the human body to the depth of an inch, while the visible rays are reflected at the surface. And it has been known to photographers for fifty years that this light—easily isolated by dispersion through prisms—will act on a sensitized plate in an utterly dark room."

"Granted," I said. "But how about the second question? How can you see by this light?"

"There you have me," he answered. "It will need a quicker development than any now known to photography—a traveling film, for instance, that will show the picture of an iceberg or a ship before it is too late to avoid it—a traveling film sensitized by a quicker acting chemical than any now used."

"Why not puzzle it out?" I asked. "It would be a wonderful invention."

"I am too old," he answered dreamily. "My life work is about done. But other and younger men will take it up. We have made great strides in optics. The moving picture is a fact. Colored photographs are possible. The ultraviolet microscope shows us objects hitherto invisible because smaller than the wave length of visible light. We shall ultimately use this light to see through opaque objects. We shall see colors never imagined by the human mind, but which have existed since the beginning of light.

"We shall see new hues in the sunset, in the rainbow, in the flowers and foliage of forest and field. We may possibly see creatures in the air above never seen before.

"We shall certainly see creatures from the depths of the sea, where visible light cannot reach—creatures whose substance is of such a nature that it will not respond to the light it has never been exposed to—a substance which is absolutely transparent because it will not absorb, and appear black; will not reflect, and show a color of some kind; and will not refract, and distort objects seen through it."

"What!" I exclaimed. "Do you think there are invisible creatures?"

He looked gravely at me for a moment, then said: "You know that there are sounds that are inaudible to the human ear because of their too rapid vibration, others that are audible to some, but not to all. There are men who cannot hear the chirp of a cricket, the tweet of a bird, or the creaking of a wagon wheel.

"You know that there are electric currents much stronger in voltage than is necessary to kill us, but of wave frequency so rapid that the human tissue will not respond, and we can receive such currents without a shock. And *I know*"—he spoke with vehemence—"that there are creatures in the deep sea of color invisible to the human eye, for I have not only felt such a creature, but seen its photograph taken by the ultraviolet light."

"Tell me," I asked breathlessly. "Creatures solid, but invisible?"

"Creatures solid, and invisible because absolutely transparent. It is long since I have told the yarn. People would not believe me, and it was so horrible an experience that I have tried to forget it. However, if you care for it, and are willing to lose your sleep to-night, I'll give it to you."

He reached for a pipe, filled it, and began to smoke; and as he smoked and talked, some of the glamor and polish of the successful artist and clubman left him. He was an old sailor, spinning a yarn.

"It was about thirty years ago," he began, "or, to be explicit, twenty-nine years this coming August, at the time of the great Java earthquake. You've heard of it—how it killed seventy thousand people, thirty thousand of whom were drowned by the tidal wave.

"It was a curious phenomenon; Krakatoa Island, a huge conical mountain rising from the bottom of Sunda Strait, went out of existence, while in Java a mountain chain was leveled, and up from the bowels of the earth came an iceberg—as you might call it—that floated a hundred miles on a stream of molten lava before melting.

"I was not there; I was two hundred miles to the sou'west, first mate of one of those old-fashioned, soft-pine, centerboard barkentines—three sticks the same length, you know—with the mainmast stepped on the port side of the keel to make room for the centerboard—a craft that would neither stay, nor wear, nor scud, nor heave to, like a decent vessel.

"But she had several advantages; she was new, and well painted, deck, top-sides, and bottom. Hence her light timbers and planking were not water-soaked. She was fastened with 'trunnels,' not spikes and bolts, and hemp rigged.

"Perhaps there was not a hundredweight of iron aboard of her, while her hemp rigging, though heavier than water, was lighter than wire rope, and so, when we were hit by the back wash of that tidal wave, we did not sink, even though butts were started from one end to the other of the flimsy hull, and all hatches were ripped off.

"I have called it the back wash, yet we may have had a tidal wave of our own; for, though we had no knowledge of the frightful catastrophe at Java, still there had been for days several submarine earthquakes all about us, sending fountains of water, steam bubbles, and mud from the sea bed into the air.

"As the soundings were over two thousand fathoms in that neighborhood, you can imagine the seismic forces at work beneath us. There had been no wind for days, and no sea, except the agitation caused by the upheavals. The sky was a dull mud color, and the sun looked like nothing but a dark, red ball, rising day by day in the east, to move overhead and set in the west. The air was hot, sultry, and stifling, and I had difficulty in keeping the men—a big crew—at work.

"The conditions would try anybody's temper, and I had my own troubles. There was a passenger on board, a big, fat, highly educated German—a scientist and explorer—whom we had taken aboard at some little town on the West Australian coast, and who was to leave us at Batavia, where he could catch a steamer for Germany.

"He had a whole laboratory with him, with scientific instruments that I didn't know the names of, with maps he had made, stuffed beasts and birds he had killed, and a few live ones which he kept in cages and attended to himself in the empty hold; for we were flying light, you know, without even ballast aboard, and bound to Batavia for a cargo.

"It was after a few eruptions from the bottom of the sea that he got to be a nuisance; he was keenly interested in the strange dead fish and nondescript creatures that had been thrown up. He declared them new, unknown to science, and wore out my patience with entreaties to haul them aboard for examination and classification.

"I obliged him for a time, until the decks stank with dead fish, and the men got mutinous. Then I refused to advance the interests of science any farther, and, in spite of his excitement and pleadings, refused to litter the decks any more. But he got all he wanted of the unclassified and unknown before long.

"Tidal wave, you know, is a name we give to any big wave, and it has no necessary connection with the tides. It may be the big third wave of a series—just a little bigger than usual; it may be the ninth, tenth, and eleventh waves merged into one huge comber by uneven wind pressure; it may be the back wash from an earthquake that depresses the nearest coast, and it may be—as I think it was in our case—a wave sent out by an upheaval from the sea bed. At any rate, we got it, and we got it just after a tremendous spouting of water and mud, and a thick cloud of steam on the northern horizon.

"We saw a seeming rise to the horizon, as though caused by refraction, but which soon eliminated refraction as a cause by its becoming visible in its details—its streaks of water and mud, its irregular upper edge, the occasional combers that appeared on this edge, and the terrific speed of its approach. It was a wave, nothing else, and coming at forty knots at least.

"There was little that we could do; there was no wind, and we headed about west, showing our broadside; yet I got the men at the downhauls, clewlines, and stripping lines of the lighter kites; but before a man could leave the deck to furl, that moving mountain hit us, and buried us on our beam ends just as I had time to sing out: 'Lash yourselves, every man.'

"Then I needed to think of my own safety and passed a turn of the mizzen gaff-topsail downhaul about me, belaying to a pin as the cataclysm hit us. For the next two minutes—although it seemed an hour, I did not speak, nor breathe, nor think, unless my instinctive grip on the turns of the downhaul on the pin may have been an index of thought. I was under water; there was roaring in my ears, pain in my lungs, and terror in my heart.

"Then there came a lessening of the turmoil, a momentary quiet, and I roused up, to find the craft floating on her side, about a third out of water, but apt to turn bottom up at any moment from the weight of the water-soaked gear and canvas, which will sink, you know, when wet.

"I was hanging in my bight of rope from a belaying pin, my feet clear of the perpendicular deck, and my ears tortured by the sound of men overboard crying for help—men who had not lashed themselves. Among them I knew was the skipper, a mild-mannered little fellow, and the second mate, an incompetent tough from Portsmouth, who had caused me lots of trouble by his abuse of the men and his depending upon me to stand by him.

"Nothing could be done for them; they were adrift on the back wall of a moving mountain that towered thirty degrees above the horizon to port; and another moving mountain, as big as the first, was coming on from starboard—caused by the tumble into the sea of the uplifted water.

"Did you ever fall overboard in a full suit of clothes? If you did, you know the mighty exercise of strength required to climb out. I was a strong, healthy man at the time, but never in my life was I so tested. I finally got a grip on the belaying pin and rested; then, with an effort that caused me physical pain, I got my right foot up to the pinrail and rested again; then, perhaps more by mental strength than physical—for I loved life and wanted to live—I hooked my right foot over the rail, reached higher on the rope, rested again, and finally hove myself up to the mizzen rigging, where I sat for a few moments to get my breath, and think, and look around.

"Forward, I saw men who had lashed themselves to the starboard rail, and they were struggling, as I had struggled, to get up to the horizontal side of the vessel. They succeeded, but at the time I had no use for them. Sailors will obey orders, if they understand the orders, but this was an exigency outside the realm of mere seamanship.

"Men were drowning off to port; men, like myself, were climbing up to temporary safety afforded by the topsides of a craft on her beam ends; and aft, in the alleyway, was the German professor, unlashed, but safe and secure in his narrow confines, one leg through a cabin window, and both hands gripping the rail, while he bellowed like a bull, not for himself, however—but for his menagerie in the empty hold.

"There was small chance for the brutes—smaller than for ourselves, left on the upper rail of an over-turned craft, and still smaller than the chance of the poor devils off to port, some of whom had gripped the half-submerged top-hamper, and were calling for help.

"We could not help them; she was a Yankee craft, and there was not a life buoy or belt on board; and who, with another big wave coming, would swim down to looward with a line?

"Landsmen, especially women and boys, have often asked me why a wooden ship, filled with water, sinks, even though not weighted with cargo. Some sailors have pondered over it, too, knowing that a small boat, built of wood, and fastened with nails, will float if water-logged.

"But the answer is simple. Most big craft are built of oak or hard pine, and fastened together with iron spikes and bolts—sixty tons at least to a three-hundred-ton schooner. After a year or two this hard, heavy wood becomes water-soaked, and, with the iron bolts and spikes, is heavier than water, and will sink when the hold is flooded.

"This craft of ours was like a small boat—built of soft light wood, with trunnels instead of bolts, and no iron on board except the anchors and one capstan. As a result, though ripped, twisted, broken, and disintegrated, she still floated even on her beam ends.

"But the soaked hemp rigging and canvas might be enough to drag the craft down, and with this fear in my mind I acted quickly. Singing out to the men to hang on, I made my way aft to where we had an ax, lodged in its beckets on the after house. With this I attacked the mizzen lanyards, cutting everything clear, then climbed forward to the main.

"Hard as I worked I had barely cut the last lanyard when that second wave loomed up and crashed down on us. I just had time to slip into the bight of a rope, and save myself; but I had to give up the ax; it slipped from my hands and slid down to the port scuppers.

"That second wave, in its effect, was about the same as the first, except that it righted the craft. We were buried, choked, and half drowned; but when the wave had passed on, the main and mizzenmasts, unsupported by the rigging that I had cut away, snapped cleanly about three feet above the deck, and the broad, flat-bottomed craft straightened up, lifting the weight of the foremast and its gear, and lay on an even keel, with foresail, staysail, and jib set, the fore gaff-topsail, flying jib, and jib-topsail clewed down and the wreck of the masts bumping against the port side.

"We floated, but with the hold full of water, and four feet of it on deck amidships that surged from one rail to the other as the craft rolled, pouring over and coming back. All hatches were ripped off, and our three boats were carried away from their chocks on the house.

"Six men were clearing themselves from their lashings at the fore rigging, and three more, who had gone overboard with the first sea, and had caught the upper gear to be lifted as the craft righted, were coming down, while the professor still declaimed from the alley.

"'Hang on all,' I yelled; 'there's another sea coming.'

"It came, but passed over us without doing any more damage, and though a fourth, fifth, and sixth followed, each was of lesser force than the last, and finally it was safe to leave the rail and wade about, though we still rolled rails under in what was left of the turmoil.

"Luckily, there was no wind, though I never understood why, for earthquakes are usually accompanied by squalls. However, even with wind, our canvas would have been no use to us; for, waterlogged as we were, we couldn't have made a knot an hour, nor could we have steered, even with all sail set. All we could hope for was the appearance of some craft that would tow the ripped and shivered hull to port, or at least take us off.

"So, while I searched for the ax, and the professor searched into the depths under the main hatch for signs of his menagerie—all drowned, surely—the remnant of the crew lowered the foresail and jibs, stowing them as best they could.

"I found the ax, and found it just in time; for I was attacked by what could have been nothing but a small-sized sea serpent, that had been hove up to the surface and washed aboard us. It was only about six feet long, but it had a mouth like a bulldog, and a row of spikes along its back that could have sawed a man's leg off.

"I managed to kill it before it harmed me, and chucked it overboard against the protests of the professor, who averred that I took no interest in science.

"'No, I don't,' I said to him. 'I've other things to think of. And you, too. You'd better go below and clean up your instruments, or you'll find them ruined by salt water.'

"He looked sorrowfully and reproachfully at me, and started to wade aft; but he halted at the forward companion, and turned, for a scream of agony rang out from the forecastle deck, where the men were coming in from the jibs, and I saw one of them writhing on his back, apparently in a fit, while the others stood wonderingly around.

"The forecastle deck was just out of water, and there was no wash; but in spite of this, the wriggling, screaming man slid head-first along the break and plunged into the water on the main deck.

"I scrambled forward, still carrying the ax, and the men tumbled down into the water after the man; but we could not get near him. We could see him under water, feebly moving, but not swimming; and yet he shot this way and that faster than a man ever swam; and once, as he passed near me, I noticed a gaping wound in his neck, from which the blood was flowing in a stream—a stream like a current, which did not mix with the water and discolor it.

"Soon his movements ceased, and I waded toward him; but he shot swiftly away from me, and I did not follow, for something cold, slimy, and firm touched my hand—something in the water, but which I could not see.

"I floundered back, still holding the ax, and sang out to the men to keep away from the dead man; for he was surely dead by now. He lay close to the break of the topgallant forecastle, on the starboard side; and as the men mustered around me I gave one my ax, told the rest to secure others, and to chop away the useless wreck pounding our port side— useless because it was past all seamanship to patch up that basketlike hull, pump it out, and raise jury rigging.

"While they were doing it, I secured a long pike pole from its beckets, and, joined by the professor, cautiously approached the body prodding ahead of me.

"As I neared the dead man, the pike pole was suddenly torn from my grasp, one end sank to the deck, while the other raised above the water; then it slid upward, fell, and floated close to me. I seized it again and turned to the professor.

"'What do you make of this, Herr Smidt?' I asked. 'There is something down there that we cannot see—something that killed that man. See the blood?'

"He peered closely at the dead man, who looked curiously distorted and shrunken, four feet under water. But the blood no longer was a thin stream issuing from his neck; it was gathered into a misshapen mass about two feet away from his neck.

"'Nonsense,' he answered. 'Something alive which we cannot see is contrary to all laws of physics. Der man must have fallen und hurt himself, which accounts for der bleeding. Den he drowned in der water. Do you see?—mine Gott! What iss?'

"He suddenly went under water himself, and dropping the pike pole, I grabbed him by the collar and braced myself. Something was pulling him away from me, but I managed to get his head out, and he spluttered:

"'Help! Holdt on to me. Something haf my right foot.'

"'Lend a hand here,' I yelled to the men, and a few joined me, grabbing him by his clothing. Together we pulled against the invisible force, and finally all of us went backward, professor and all, nearly to drown ourselves before regaining our feet. Then, as the agitated water smoothed, I distinctly saw the mass of red move slowly forward and disappear in the darkness under the forecastle deck.

"'You were right, mine friend,' said the professor, who, in spite of his experience, held his nerve. 'Dere is something invisible in der water—something dangerous, something which violates all laws of physics und optics. Oh, mine foot, how it hurts!'

"'Get aft,' I answered, 'and find out what ails it. And you fellows,' I added to the men, 'keep away from the forecastle deck. Whatever it is, it has gone under it.'

"Then I grabbed the pike pole again, cautiously hooked the barb into the dead man's clothing, and, assisted by the men, pulled him aft to the poop, where the professor had preceded, and was examining his ankle. There was a big, red wale around it, in the middle of which was a huge blood blister. He pricked it with his knife, then rearranged his stocking and joined us as we lifted the body.

"'Great God, sir!' exclaimed big Bill, the bosun. 'Is that Frank? I wouldn't know him.'

"Frank, the dead man, had been strong, robust, and full-blooded. But he bore no resemblance to his living self. He lay there, shrunken, shortened, and changed, a look of agony on his emaciated face, and his hands clenched—not extended like those of one drowned.

"'I thought drowned men swelled up,' ventured one of the men.

"'He was not drowned,' said Herr Smidt. 'He was sucked dry, like a lemon. Perhaps in his whole body there is not an ounce of blood, nor lymph, nor fluid of any kind.'

"I secured an iron belaying pin, tucked it inside his shirt, and we hove him overboard at once; for, in the presence of this horror, we were not in the mood for a burial service. There we were, eleven men on a water-logged hulk, adrift on a heaving, greasy sea, with a dark-red sun showing through a muddy sky above, and an invisible *thing* forward that might seize any of us at any moment it chose, in the water or out; for Frank had been caught and dragged down.

"Still, I ordered the men, cook, steward, and all, to remain on the poop and—the galley being forward—to expect no hot meals, as we could subsist for a time on the cold, canned food in the storeroom and lazaret.

"Because of an early friction between the men and the second mate, the mild-mannered and peace-loving skipper had forbidden the crew to wear sheath knives; but in this exigency I overruled the edict. While the professor went down into his flooded room to doctor his ankle and attend to his instruments, I raided the slop chest, and armed every man of us with a sheath knife and belt; for while we could not see the creature, we could feel it—and a knife is better than a gun in a hand-to-hand fight.

"Then we sat around, waiting, while the sky grew muddier, the sun darker, and the northern horizon lighter with a reddish glow that was better than the sun. It was the Java earthquake, but we did not know it for a long time.

"Soon the professor appeared and announced that his instruments were in good condition, and stowed high on shelves above the water.

"'I must resensitize my plates, however,' he said. 'Der salt water has spoiled them; but mine camera merely needs to dry out; und mine telescope, und mine static machine und Leyden jars—why, der water did not touch them.'

"'Well,' I answered. 'That's all right. But what good are they in the face of this emergency? Are you thinking of photographing anything now?'

"'Perhaps. I haf been thinking some.'

"'Have you thought out what that creature is—forward, there?'

"'Partly. It is some creature thrown up from der bottom of der sea, und washed on board by der wave. Light, like wave motion, ends at a certain depth, you know; und we have over twelve thousand feet beneath us. At that depth dere is absolute darkness, but we know that creatures live down dere, und fight, und eat, und die.'

"'But what of it? Why can't we see that thing?'

"'Because, in der ages that haf passed in its evolution from der original moneron, it has never been exposed to light—I mean visible light, der light that contains der seven colors of der spectrum. Hence it may not respond to der three properties of visible light—reflection, which would give it a color of some kind; absorption, which would make it appear black; or refraction, which, in der absence of der other two, would distort things seen through it. For it would be transparent, you know.'

"'But what can be done?' I asked helplessly, for I could not understand at the time what he meant.

"'Nothing, except that der next man attacked must use his knife. If he cannot see der creature, he can feel it. Und perhaps—I do not know yet—perhaps, in a way, we may see it—its photograph.'

"I looked blankly at him, thinking he might have gone crazy, but he continued.

"'You know,' he said, 'that objects too small to be seen by the microscope, because smaller than der amplitude of der shortest wave of visible light, can be seen when exposed to der ultraviolet light—der dark light beyond der spectrum? Und you know that this light is what acts der most in photography? That it exposes on a sensitized plate new stars in der heavens invisible to der eye through the strongest telescope?'

"'Don't know anything about it,' I answered. 'But if you can find a way out of this scrape we're in, go ahead.'

"'I must think,' he said dreamily. 'I haf a rock-crystal lens which is permeable to this light, und which I can place in mine camera. I must have a concave mirror, not of glass, which is opaque to this light, but of metal.'

"'What for?' I asked.

"'To throw der ultraviolet light on der beast. I can generate it with mine static machine.'

"'How will one of our lantern reflectors do? They are of polished tin, I think.'

"'Good! I can repolish one.'

"We had one deck lantern larger than usual, with a metallic reflector that concentrated the light into a beam, much as do the present day searchlights. This I procured from the lazaret, and he pronounced it available. Then he disappeared, to tinker up his apparatus.

"Night came down, and I lighted three masthead lights, to hoist at the fore to inform any passing craft that we were not under command; but, as I would not send a man forward on that job, I went myself, carefully feeling my way with the pike pole. Luckily, I escaped contact with the creature, and returned to the poop, where we had a cold supper of canned cabin stores.

"The top of the house was dry, but it was cold, especially so as we were all drenched to the skin. The steward brought up all the blankets there were in the cabin—for even a wet blanket is better than none at all—but there were not enough to go around, and one man volunteered, against my advice, to go forward and bring aft bedding from the forecastle.

"He did not come back; we heard his yell, that finished with a gurgle; but in that pitch black darkness, relieved only by the red glow from the north, not one of us dared to venture to his rescue. We knew that he would be dead, anyhow, before we could get to him; so we stood watch, sharing the blankets we had when our time came to sleep.

"It was a wretched night that we spent on the top of that after house. It began to rain before midnight, the heavy drops coming down almost in solid waves; then came wind, out of the south, cold and biting, with real waves, that rolled even over the house, forcing us to lash ourselves. The red glow to the north was hidden by the rain and spume, and, to add to our discomfort, we were showered with ashes, which, even though the surface wind was from the south, must have been brought from the north by an upper air current.

"We did not find the dead man when the faint daylight came; and so could not tell whether or not he had used his knife. His body must have washed over the rail with a sea, and we hoped the invisible killer had gone, too. But we hoped too much. With courage born of this hope a man went forward to lower the masthead lights, prodding his way with the pike pole.

"We watched him closely, the pole in one hand, his knife in the other. But he went under at the fore rigging without even a yell, and the pole went with him, while we could see, even at the distance and through the disturbed water, that his arms were close to his sides, and that he made no movement, except for the quick darting to and fro. After a few moments, however, the pike pole floated to the surface, but the man's body, drained, no doubt, of its buoyant fluids, remained on the deck.

"It was an hour later, with the pike pole for a feeler, before we dared approach the body, hook on to it, and tow it aft. It resembled that of the first victim, a skeleton clothed with skin, with the same look of horror on the face. We buried it like the other, and held to the poop, still drenched by the downpour of rain, hammered by the seas, and choked by ashes from the sky.

"As the shower of ashes increased it became dark as twilight, and though the three lights aloft burned out at about midday, I forbade a man to go forward to lower them, contenting myself with a turpentine flare lamp that I brought up from the lazaret, and filled, ready to show if the lights of a craft came in view. Before the afternoon was half gone it was dark as night, and down below, up to his waist in water, the German professor was working away.

"He came up at supper time, humming cheerfully to himself, and announced that he had replaced his camera lens with the rock crystal, that the lantern, with its reflector and a blue spark in the focus, made an admirable instrument for throwing the invisible rays on the beast, and that he was all ready, except that his plates, which he had resensitized— with some phosphorescent substance that I forget the name of, now— must have time to dry. And then, he needed some light to work by when the time came, he explained.

"'Also another victim,' I suggested bitterly; for he had not been on deck when the last two men had died.

"'I hope not,' he said. 'When we can see, it may be possible to stir him up by throwing things forward; then when he moves der water we can take shots.'

"'Better devise some means of killing him,' I answered. 'Shooting won't do, for water stops a bullet before it goes a foot into it.'

"'Der only way I can think of,' he responded, 'is for der next man—you hear me all, you men—to stick your knife at the end of the blood—where it collects in a lump. Dere is der creature's stomach, and a vital spot.'

"'Remember this, boys,' I laughed, thinking of the last poor devil, with his arms pinioned to his side. 'When you've lost enough blood to see it in a lump, stab for it.'

"But my laugh was answered by a shriek. A man lashed with a turn of rope around his waist to the stump of the mizzenmast, was writhing and heaving on his back, while he struck with his knife, apparently at his own body. With my own knife in my hand I sprang toward him, and felt for what had seized him. It was something cold, and hard, and leathery, close to his waist.

"Carefully gauging my stroke, I lunged with the knife, but I hardly think it entered the invisible fin, or tail, or paw of the monster; but it moved away from the screaming man, and the next moment I received a blow in the face that sent me aft six feet, flat on my back. Then came unconsciousness.

"When I recovered my senses the remnant of the crew were around me, but the man was gone—dragged out of the bight of the rope that had held him against the force of breaking seas, and down to the flooded main deck, to die like the others. It was too dark to see, or do anything; so, when I could speak I ordered all hands but one into the flooded cabin where, in the upper berths and on the top of the table, were a few dry spots.

"I filled and lighted a lantern, and gave it to the man on watch with instructions to hang it to the stump of the mizzen and to call his relief at the end of four hours. Then, with doors and windows closed, we went to sleep, or tried to go to sleep. I succeeded first, I think, for up to the last of consciousness I could hear the mutterings of the men; when I awakened, they were all asleep, and the cabin clock, high above the water, told me that, though it was still dark, it was six in the morning.

"I went on deck; the lantern still burned at the stump of mizzenmast but the lookout was gone. He had not lived long enough to be relieved, as I learned by going below and finding that no one had been called.

"We were but six, now—one sailor and the bos'n, the cook and steward, the professor and myself."

The old artist paused, while he refilled and lighted his pipe. I noticed that the hand that held the match shook perceptibly, as though the memories of that awful experience had affected his nerves. I know that the recital had affected mine; for I joined him in a smoke, my hands shaking also.

"Why," I asked, after a moment of silence, "if it was a deep-sea creature, did it not die from the lesser pressure at the surface?"

"Why do not men die on the mountaintops?" he answered. "Or up in balloons? The record is seven miles high, I think; but they lived. They suffered from cold, and from lack of oxygen—that is, no matter how fast, or deeply they breathed, they could not get enough. But the lack of pressure did not trouble them; the human body can adjust itself.

"Conversely, however, an increase of pressure may be fatal. A man dragged down more than one hundred and fifty feet may be crushed; and a surface fish sent to the bottom of the sea may die from the pressure. It is simple; it is like the difference between a weight lifted from us and a weight added."

"Did this thing kill any more men?" I asked.

"All but the professor and myself, and it almost killed me. Look here."

He removed his cravat and collar, pulled down his shirt, and exposed two livid scars about an inch in diameter, and two apart.

"I lost all the blood I could spare through those two holes," he said, as he readjusted his apparel; "but I saved enough to keep me alive."

"Go on with the yarn," I asked. "I promise you I will not sleep to-night."

"Perhaps I will not sleep myself," he answered, with a mournful smile. "Some things should be forgotten, but as I have told you this much I may as well finish, and be done with it.

"It was partly due to a sailor's love for tobacco, partly to our cold, drenched condition. A sailor will starve quietly, but go crazy if deprived of his smoke. This is so well known at sea that a skipper, who will not hesitate to sail from port with rotten or insufficient food for his men, will not dare take a chance without a full supply of tobacco in the slop chest.

"But our slop chest was under water, and the tobacco utterly useless. I did not use it at the time, but I fished some out for the others. It did not do; it would not dry out to smoke, and the salt in it made it unfit to chew. But the bos'n had an upper bunk in the forward house, in which was a couple of pounds of navy plug, and he and the sailor talked this over until their craving for a smoke overcame their fear of death.

"Of course, by this time, all discipline was ended, and all my commands and entreaties went for nothing. They sharpened their knives, and, agreeing to go forward, one on the starboard rail, the other on the port, and each to come to the other's aid if called, they went up into the darkness of ashes and rain. I opened my room window, which overlooked the main deck, but could see nothing.

"Yet I could hear; I heard two screams for help, one after the other—one from the starboard side, the other from the port, and knew that they were caught. I closed the window, for nothing could be done. What manner of thing it was that could grab two men so far apart nearly at the same time was beyond all imagining.

"I talked to the steward and cook, but found small comfort. The first was a Jap, the other a Chinaman, and they were the old-fashioned kind—what they could not see with their eyes, they could not believe. Both thought that all those men who had met death had either drowned or died by falling. Neither understood—and, in fact, I did not myself—the theories of Herr Smidt. He had stopped his cheerful humming to himself now, and was very busy with his instruments.

"'This thing,' I said to him, 'must be able to see in the dark. It certainly could not have heard those two men, over the noise of the wind, sea, and rain.'

"'Why not?' he answered, as he puttered with his wires. 'Cats and owls can see in the dark, und the accepted explanation is that by their power of enlarging der pupils they admit more light to the retina. But that explanation never satisfied me. You haf noticed, haf you not, that a cat's eyes shine in der dark, but only when der cat is looking at you?— that is, when it looks elsewhere you do not see der shiny eyes.'

"'Yes,' I answered, 'I have noticed that.'

"'A cat's eyes are searchlights, but they send forth a visible light, such as is generated by fireflies, und some fish. Und dere are fish in der upper tributaries of der Amazon which haf four eyes, der two upper of which are searchlights, der two lower of which are organs of percipience or vision. But visible light is not der only light. It is possible that the creature out on deck generates the invisible light, and can see by it.'

"'But what does it all amount to?' I asked impatiently.

"'I haf told you,' he answered calmly. 'Der creature may live in an atmosphere of ultraviolet light, which I can generate mineself. When mine plates dry, und it clears off so I can see what I am doing, I may get a picture of it. When we know what it is, we may find means of killing it.'

"'God grant that you succeed,' I answered fervently. 'It has killed enough of us.'

"But, as I said, the thing killed all but the professor and myself. And it came about through the other reason I mentioned—our cold, drenched condition. If there is anything an Oriental loves above his ancestors, it is his stomach; and the cold, canned food was palling upon us all. We had a little light through the downpour of ashes and rain about mid-day, and the steward and cook began talking about hot coffee.

"We had the turpentine torch for heating water, and some coffee, high and dry on a shelf in the steward's storeroom, but not a pot, pan, or cooking utensil of any kind in the cabin. So these two poor heathen, against my expostulations—somewhat faint, I admit, for the thought of hot coffee took away some of my common sense— went out on the deck and waded forward, waist-deep in the water, muddy now, from the downfall of ashes.

"I could see them as they entered the galley to get the coffeepot, but, though I stared from my window until the blackness closed down, I did not see them come out. Nor did I hear even a squeal. The thing must have been in the galley.

"Night came on, and, with its coming, the wind and rain ceased, though there was still a slight shower of ashes. But this ended toward midnight, and I could see stars overhead and a clear horizon. Sleep, in my nervous, overwrought condition, was impossible; but the professor, after the bright idea of using the turpentine torch to dry out his plates, had gone to his fairly dry berth, after announcing his readiness to take snapshots about the deck in the morning.

"But I roused him long before morning. I roused him when I saw through my window the masthead and two side lights of a steamer approaching from the starboard, still about a mile away. I had not dared to go up and rig that lantern at the mizzen stump; but now I nerved myself to go up with the torch, the professor following with his instruments.

"'You cold-blooded crank,' I said to him, as I waved the torch. 'I admire your devotion to science, but are you waiting for that thing to get me?'

"He did not answer, but rigged his apparatus on the top of the cabin. He had a Wimshurst machine—to generate a blue spark, you know—and this he had attached to the big deck light, from which he had removed the opaque glass. Then he had his camera, with its rock-crystal lens.

"He trained both forward, and waited, while I waved the torch, standing near the stump with a turn of rope around me for safety's sake in case the thing seized me; and to this idea I added the foolish hope, aroused by the professor's theories, that the blinding light of the torch would frighten the thing away from me as it does wild animals.

"But in this last I was mistaken. No sooner was there an answering blast of a steam whistle, indicating that the steamer had seen the torch, than something cold, wet, leathery, and slimy slipped around my neck. I dropped the torch, and drew my knife, while I heard the whir of the static machine as the professor turned it.

"'Use your knife, mine friend,' he called. 'Use your knife, und reach for any blood what you see.'

"I knew better than to call for help, and I had little chance to use the knife. Still, I managed to keep my right hand, in which I held it, free, while that cold, leathery thing slipped farther around my neck and waist. I struck as I could, but could make no impression; and soon I felt another stricture around my legs, which brought me on my back.

"Still another belt encircled me, and, though I had come up warmly clad in woolen shirts and monkey jacket, I felt these garments being torn away from me. Then I was dragged forward, but the turn of rope had slipped down toward my waist, and I was merely bent double.

"And all the time that German was whirling his machine, and shouting to strike for any blood I saw. But I saw none. I felt it going, however. Two spots on my chest began to smart, then burn as though hot irons were piercing me. Frantically I struck, right and left, sometimes at the coils encircling me, again in the air. Then all became dark.

"I AWAKENED IN A STATEROOM berth, too weak to lift my hands, with the taste of brandy in my mouth and the professor standing over me with a bottle in his hand.

"'Ach, it is well,' he said. 'You will recover. You haf merely lost blood, but you did the right thing. You struck with your knife at the blood, and you killed the creature. I was right. Heart, brain, und all vital parts were in der stomach.'

"'Where are we now?' I asked, for I did not recognize the room.

"'On board der steamer. When you got on your feet und staggered aft, I knew you had killed him, and gave you my assistance. But you fainted away. Then we were taken off. Und I haf two or three beautiful negatives, which I am printing. They will be a glorious contribution to der scientific world.'

"I was glad that I was alive, yet not alive enough to ask any more questions. But next day he showed me the photographs he had printed."

"In Heaven's name, what was it?" I asked excitedly, as the old artist paused to empty and refill his pipe.

"Nothing but a giant squid, or octopus. Except that it was bigger than any ever seen before, and invisible to the eye, of course. Did you ever read Hugo's terrible story of Gilliat's fight with a squid?"

I had, and nodded.

"Hugo's imagination could not give him a creature—no matter how formidable—larger than one of four feet stretch. This one had three tentacles around me, two others gripped the port and starboard pin-rails, and three were gripping the stump of the mainmast. It had a reach of forty feet, I should think, comparing it with the beam of the craft.

"But there was one part of each picture, ill defined and missing. My knife and right hand were not shown. They were buried in a dark lump, which could be nothing but the blood from my veins. Unconscious, but still struggling, I had struck into the soft body of the monster, and struck true."

MORGAN ROBERTSON

NOAH'S ARK

S am Rogers told me the story that follows, as we sat in the coils
of the foremain and topsail braces—easy chairs aboard ship—and,
sheltered from the blast of wind and spume by the high-weather rail,
killed time in the night-watch by yarn-spinning.

For neither of us had a wheel or lookout that night; and as he and
I were the only Americans in the forward end of the ship, we naturally
sought each other for communion and counsel—he, a tall, straight,
and slim man of fifty, an ex-man-of-war's man; I, a boy, beginning the
battle of life.

Sam was an inveterate reader; and, while his diction embraced a
choice stock of profanity, which he used when aroused, it also expressed
itself in the choicest of English, his sentences full of commas, semicolons,
and periods. He reeled off his stories as though reading from a book.

I had mentioned my boyish terror of bears, wolves, and other
bugaboos of childhood, and Sam responded with his yarn. Here it is,
just as he told it:

"She was a menagerie ship—Noah's Arks, as we called them. One of
these craft that sail out to the Orient in ballast; and, stopping at Anjer
Point for monkeys; Calcutta, Bombay, and Rangoon for elephants,
tigers, lions, and cobras; Cape Town for orang-utans and African
snakes, and over at Montevideo and Rio for wild hogs, pythons, boa-
constrictors, porcupines, and other South American jungle denizens.

"I don't know just where this craft had been to get the assorted
cargo that I saw when I shipped for the run from Rio to New York;
but I found a mess of trouble in that hold that made me think a lot,
and a limited skipper and mates that made me worry a lot. For they
had stowed a mad elephant under the fore-hatch; and this gentleman
kept all hands awake when he liked, snorting and trumpeting, with no
regard for eight bells or the watch below.

"There were Hindoo keepers aboard, but these fellows are useless in
cold weather; they shrivel up and move slowly, paralyzed by the cold.
We got the cold up in the north latitudes, just above the trades; and it
was about this time that the trouble began.

"We had the ordinary mixed crew of a Yankee ship—only, this craft
was a bark; and we had the usual bull-headed and ignorant Yankee
skipper and mates; men with no understanding of human or brute

nature; men who would rather hit you than listen to your proposition of peace. They hit us all, and got us into a condition of mind that discounted that of the elephant under the hatch.

"Besides that elephant there were stowed in that hold cages containing wolves, hyenas, wild hogs, wild asses, monkeys, porcupines, and zebras. There were three or four cages full of poisonous snakes, one variety of which I recognized, the curse of India—the hooded cobra. Then there was a big python, picked up at Rio, and a boa-constrictor, taken aboard at one of the Pacific islands.

"There was a huge Nubian lion; a big, striped Bengal tiger; a hippopotamus, and a rhinoceros, to complete the list. I tell you, it made me creepy to go down among them, as we had to on occasions, to wash down.

"The elephant was moored to a stanchion by a short length of chain shackled around his hind leg, but it gave him a radius of action equal to his length and that of his hind leg and trunk. This precluded our using the fore-hatch to reach the hold, so we used the main-hatch; and, as there was daily use of it, this hatch was fitted with steps, and always kept open, even in bad weather.

"The immediate cause of the trouble was the carrying away of the foretop-gallant-yard, due to rotten halyards, and braces and lifts, when we were scudding before a gale off Hatteras. The yard came down on the whirl, but when it hit the deck it hit like a pile-driver—a straight, perpendicular blow—directly over the partners that held the upper end of the stanchion to which that crazy elephant was moored.

"It weakened it. We heard the big brute's protest, and then we heard the crash as he carried away the stanchion.

"Then we heard other noises as he raced aft among the cages—the mad squealing of the elephant, the growling and roaring of the lion and the tiger, the barking of the wolves and hyenas, the gruntings of the wild hogs, the heehaws of the wild asses and zebras, and the terrible, mumbling snorts of the hippopotamus and rhinoceros, as their cages were upset and destroyed.

"That mad elephant smashed them all, as we learned when the whole bunch, according to their acceptance of the situation, appeared on deck, growling or whining, looking for something to do or to kill. All hands were up, and we all took to the rigging, even the skipper and mates and the man at the wheel.

"The ship broached to, and away went the upper spars and yards. The canvas slatted and thrashed and, one by one, the sails went to ribbons and rags; but we could not help it. Down on deck were a big yellow lion and striped tiger wandering round, swishing their tails to starboard and port, looking for trouble.

"Also a python and a boa-constrictor, a half-dozen wolves from the Russian plateaus, the zebras and wild asses, the hyenas, with their ugly faces; the porcupines, and some of the small venomous snakes. We could see them as they climbed up the steps of the main-hatch.

"Even the rhinoceros and the hippopotamus came up; but, when the mad elephant tried, the steps broke under his weight, and he remained below. Still, we had a problem.

"There wasn't a gun among us, and to go down and face those beasts with handspikes was out of the question.

"I was in the mizzen crosstrees with the skipper, the second mate, the helmsman, and a couple of Sou'wegians who had been working aft. In the maintop were the first mate and three or four of the crew, and in the foretop were the rest, all bunched together and waiting for instructions.

"The skipper gave them.

"'Go down out o' that,' he yelled, 'and drive them down the hatch!'

"But not a man moved. Who would? He told me to go over and lash the wheel amidships, and I declined, as politely as I could. The wheel was spinning back and forth, the ship rolling in the trough, and the upper spars, hanging by their gear, slatting back and forth as the ship rolled.

"Down on deck were those murderous wild beasts, nosing round, and only waiting for the chance of getting together. I told this to the skipper.

"'Right,' he said. 'Perhaps they'll kill each other.'

"This seemed possible a few minutes later, when the tiger and the lion met face to face. They glared and growled and spit, just like two huge tomcats, then they sailed into each other.

"It was a lively scrap. They fenced and dodged and nipped as they could, but their motions were too swift to give either a good chance at a bite. They were in the air half the time, on their backs the other half, and it seemed an even fight until the tiger, in one of his plunges, bumped into the python, who had been squirming around the deck.

"Now, a python is not poisonous; but, nevertheless, he has a strong grip of jaw. He closed his jaws on the tiger's nose, and then began a funny sight. The big, striped brute could not shake him off; but he backed away, snarling and screaming with rage and pain, forward round the house, and aft on the other side to the space abaft the main-hatch, the snake writhing like a whip-lash, and the tiger never making an effort to use his forepaws.

"It seemed as though hereditary fear had seized him, for with a few digs and blows he could have clawed him off. This fight ended by the writhing python getting too close to the boa-constrictor, who happened to be nosing his way across the deck amidships. In the twinkling of an eye, the boa wrapped himself around the python, and the tiger got away.

"Then, while the two big snakes thrashed around the deck, Mr. Bengal slunk away like a cat scared by a dog—his tail between his legs, and the fur on his back raised up so that it looked like that of a razor-backed hog.

"He went forward of the house to think it over, and the two snakes fought it out, while the lion, thinking that he had won the fight, roared and growled his defiance to the rest.

"He was too confident; the big rhinoceros looked him in the face, and the trouble was resumed.

"Mr. Lion charged; but the rhino lowered his head, caught him between the forepaws with his horn, and sent him flying over his head, with a big gash in his body. That was enough for the lion, king of beasts though he was.

"Leaving a trail of blood, he slunk forward of the house, and there must have met his enemy, the tiger. We could not see, but we could hear, and we knew the fight between the two was resumed.

"The snakes were thrashing it out all this time, but neither seemed to get the better of it. The boa's instincts were to crush, the python's to swallow; but this swallowing pertained also to the boa, and it came about that the boa got about three inches of the python's tail into his mouth, and later the python got a grip on the boa's tail.

"They held fast and ceased their struggles, their efforts now being centered in the desire to swallow each other. This seemed a good solution of our problem, and we wished them well.

"Meanwhile, the hyenas and the Russian wolves got mixed up, and—talk about your dog fights—you never saw anything like it. Those beasts fought and snarled and wrestled round the deck in a way to make you glad you were up aloft, out of harm's way.

"It was a strange fight; both the hyenas and the wolves are cowards, each afraid of the other. And it was only when two wolves got at a hyena, or two hyenas got at a wolf that there was any real scrapping. But it came about that these two breeds destroyed each other.

"One after the other crawled away to die from loss of blood.

"The wild asses and zebras had got busy. Something about the arrangement of the zebra's stripes must have offended the artistic sensibilities of the wild asses, for pretty soon there was a lively kicking-match going on round the deck—a zebra against a donkey, kicking out, stern to stern, like prize-fighters sparring. It was funny, the way they looked round at each other while backing up to a fresh reach.

"Now, the tiger and the lion were having it out forward of the house; the wolves and the hyenas were scrapping, as they could, two against one; the python and the cobra were trying to swallow each other, and the asses and zebras were kicking the ribs out of each other. And, as if this were not enough to complete the circus, the hippo and the rhino must get together.

"Hippo made a plunging charge upon rhino and met that formidable tusk. But the hide of a hippo is something akin to armor-plate, and there was no damage, though the big brute was lifted and turned over. He came back, and in some manner got a grip on that big horn with his teeth; and from that on, their fight was simply a wrestling-match, neither able to hurt the other.

"And over their grunts and groanings, over the noise of the wolves and hyenas, the tiger and lion, and the slatting and bumping of the broken gear against the mast, and the sounds of sea and wind, rose supreme to our ears the blatant squealing and trumpeting of that mad elephant in the 'tween-decks.

"Added to this were the insane orders to us fellows of the skipper and the two mates. They demanded that we go down and quell the disturbance. Well, we did not go down. We did other things.

"It was I who suggested to the skipper the advisability of cutting away the connections that held those spars and sails aloft, so that they would drop down and free the ship of the extra top-hamper. He was badly rattled, but accepted my suggestion; so, at his orders, men went aloft on all three masts, and soon the wreck came down, the mizzen top-hamper falling overboard and the main diving down the open main-hatch. We hoped it hit the elephant.

"It was only chance, of course; but the foretop-gallantmast, with the royal yard attached, did hit the tiger a smashing blow on the head that ended his troubles. We could see him, just clear of the forward house, with the lion at his throat. There wasn't much of it. The lion bit in; then, satisfied that he had done the job, he left the dead tiger and came aft, still bleeding from the hole between the forelegs, and pounced upon rhino, who had made that hole.

"It roused the rhino. With a mighty upheaval, he shook off the hippo and charged on the lion. But this fighter had grown wary; he dodged and jumped, growling and snarling the while, but apparently in no mood to again risk the puncturing of his hide by that upright horn.

"Meanwhile the stupid old hippo, who usually wanted nothing more than his grub and his bath, lumbered around looking for further trouble. He found it; he interfered between the wild asses and the zebras, and soon the whole bunch, both sides, were bombarding him with their hind feet. He squealed and groaned and growled, but to no end.

"They backed up to him and thumped him with their hoofs, as many as could get near him. It was a beautiful exhibition of the law of the brotherhood of man and the brotherhood of beast. Those equine propagandists of the law of the survival of the fittest kicked that poor, peaceful old hippo into a condition of coma.

"At last he lay down, with his head between his paws, and gave it up; then the kickers ceased kicking him and resumed their kicking of each other.

"By this time the python and the boa had gathered in about three feet of each other; the wolves and hyenas—two against one, understand—had reduced their number by half, and the lion was still pretending to fight the rhino.

"He still found it best to dodge that upright tusk, while his claws and teeth couldn't even scratch the rhino's impervious hide.

"Then he got it from another quarter. The porcupines had climbed up, and one was nosing round the deck, attending to his own affairs—which seemed to be nothing more than an intention to find out where he was—when he got between these two. He suddenly balled himself up, turned round a couple of times, and then fired a volley of his quills.

"They went, straight and true, right into that open hole between the lion's forelegs. He stood on his hindfeet for a moment, bellowing and roaring, while he tried to brush them out; then he slunk forward again and hid behind the house. But we heard his occasional snarls of pain.

"Meanwhile the porcupine had opened fire on the rhino, but did him no harm; and rhino was too big-minded to notice him. He lumbered round, looking for a match with something, but not finding it; even the kickers got out of his way, and the poor old hippo wandered forward to commune with the lion.

"Not finding an antagonist worthy of his horn, the rhino began nosing the two mutual-minded snakes. He tossed them 'round, and they were helpless to resist—only the rough handling seemed to induce increased swallowing power. We could see their jaws working convulsively; and inch by inch, foot by foot, they rapidly disappeared from sight.

"The rhino soon got tired and tackled the wolves and hyenas—what was left of them. They had reduced their number to two of each kind; but this was too small to admit of two against one, so they were now dodging each other, snarling bravely enough, but not fighting.

"The rhino caught a hyena on his tusk, tossed him in air, caught him as he fell, sent him flying again, and then stamped his life out. This seemed to settle the fate of the other hyena, for immediately the two remaining wolves got at him. But rhino's next victim was a wolf, which he disposed of as quickly.

"This left two cowards to fight for the supremacy; but the fight was taken out of them. They slunk apart and did not meet again.

"Now, here was the condition of things when a new factor intruded upon the problem: the lion was nursing his hurts, forward of the house, out of sight; the hippo had gone to sleep from sheer weariness and disgust; the last wolf and hyena were prowling round, avoiding each other; the python and the boa had swallowed two-thirds of each other's length; the rhino was wandering round, looking for a scrap; the kicking zebras and wild asses had grown tired and called it a draw, and the porcupines, three or four of them, had finished their inspection of their environment and had snuggled down in various places to await developments.

"The new factor was a green sea that lifted aboard amidships and flooded the waist of the ship. Of course, the quick movers of the lot got forward or aft, out of the way of the water surging back and forth across the deck; but the poor porcupines were drowned before the water ran out the scuppers. And when it had gone out, we saw what we had not seen before—the small, poisonous cobras.

"They had come up, but had kept out of sight until that sea washed them round; then, as the water shallowed on the deck, they made for the masts or the rigging and began to climb. It's hard to drown a snake, you know.

"There were at least two dozen of the reptiles, and it looked bad for us fellows aloft. Did you ever see a snake climb a rope? He goes up in a sort of wriggling spiral, wrapped loosely round it, but shifting his different sections up for a fresh grip. The other fellows climbed to the topmast-crosstrees and looked down; but the snakes stopped at the eyes of the rigging, or the tops, and rested.

"Then came a second new factor in our problem: a sea came aboard from the other side and washed about; another with the next roll, and still another. The rolls were long and heavy, and I, who had once been on a sinking ship, sensed the reason.

"'We're sinking, captain,' I said. 'That main-topgallantmast going down that hatch has punched a hole or started a butt.'

"'Maybe you're right,' he exclaimed. 'What can we do?'

"That was too hard a question at the time for a skipper to ask of a foremast-hand, so I said nothing, but did a lot of thinking. The flywheel-pump was amidships at the main fife-rail. We could not go down to it without danger from the wounded lion, the rhino, and possibly the wolf, though, with these out of the way, we might dodge or kill the cobras and fight off the hyena.

"As it was, we were caught. I suggested to the skipper that he go down the mizzentopmast-backstay, dart into his cabin, and get his rifle. Then he could pot the brutes from the forward windows. But he declined and forbade me going. I had no business in his cabin.

"I saw that he had lost his nerve. Now, when a skipper loses his nerve, he loses his rights; so I didn't hesitate to sing out to the mate in the main-topmast-crosstrees to clear away downhaul-blocks, quarter-blocks, or anything handy and heavy, and try and drop them on the lion and the rhino, the two most dangerous of the bunch. He seemed to be much in the same condition as the skipper, for he answered and passed the word forward to the fellows on the fore.

"In a few minutes things began raining down onto the deck—blocks, bulls'-eyes, and sea-boots. The bombardment raised a commotion, though none of the brutes was hit.

"Yet the sick and sore lion responded to the extent of bounding aft and mounting the poop. Here he came within range of us fellows up the mizzen, and I had the disconnected mizzen-staysail halyard-block in my hand ready for him. He gained the space abaft the house near the wheel and stood still, lashing his tail and nosing the air as though he smelled us up aloft.

"He was only about forty feet down; and when young I had been a good ball-player. I leaned over and let that block go with all my strength. It wasn't the ordinary shell-block, but a solid carving of *lignum-vitæ*;

and it fetched that lion a smash on the head that must have cracked his skull, for he sank down, then got up and wabbled, rather than walked, forward along the alley to the poop-steps.

"There he blindly fell off the poop; and the rhino, whom he had dodged on the run aft, was ready for him. It wasn't a fight. The lion was dying, and the rhino simply hastened the job, goring him relentlessly until the bleeding carcass lay still.

"Then the rhino, flushed with victory, went for the nearest brute, a wild ass, and soon he had the whole of them—asses and zebras—kicking the stomach out of him, or into him, perhaps, by the way he bellowed.

"It was funny, in a way, for they were all too quick for him; they could dodge that plunging beast with his murderous horn, and turn for a kick before he got by.

"But there was nothing funny about that water in the hold, nor in the prospective job of stopping the leak, pumping her out, and bending new canvas, in case we could get that rhinoceros out of the way. He was the only thing we feared now, for the rest were not really dangerous unless you got too close.

"We knew the wolf and the hyena would run from a man with a handspike, and the zebras and asses would run from a man without one. To make matters worse, darkness closed down. So, lashing ourselves to the crosstrees, we slept more or less sweetly until daylight.

"When we took stock of things, we knew that all was up with that bark. Her plank-sheer amidships was awash, and the water rolling in a green body from starboard to port and back again.

"The crazy elephant stood under the hatch, squealing and trumpeting in fright. He must have smashed the monkeys' cages during the night, for the rigging was dotted with chimpanzees, orangs, and the small fellows. The hyena and the wolf had gained the forecastle-deck, and stood, side by side, looking aft, with no thought of quarreling in this emergency.

"The sleepy old hippo was lumbering round in the flooded waist as though he enjoyed his salt-water bath; and the rhino was forward on the main deck, looking at the water as it washed up to him and receded. Amidships was a thick, black ring of about two feet diameter, sliding round in the wash.

"It was the two big snakes, each a sheath for the other, but each dead as a door-nail; either they had died from the strain, or the water had drowned them. The zebras and wild asses were also forward, but mostly out of sight behind the house. Not a cobra could be seen, however, and the skipper displayed sudden energy.

"'Something must be done,' he said vehemently. 'You men stay here while I make the attempt to get to the top of the forward house. If I can make it without trouble, the rest of you can follow. We must clear away the boats, for there is no saving this ship.'

"So saying, he gripped the mizzen-stay and slid down it to where it ended at a band on the main-mast just above the fife-rail. From there he dropped to the deck and made a bee-line for the starboard side of the house to avoid the rhino, who was forward on the port side.

"But the rhino saw him coming down the stay and lumbered aft into the washing-water to investigate, rounding the port corner of the house just as the skipper reached the starboard. From there he charged; and you cannot imagine the velocity of a rhino's charge. It is like that of a locomotive. The skipper scrambled on top of a water-tank alongside the house just in time to escape that tusk, and from there he got to the top, where he sat down to recover himself.

"He was a badly scared man. The rhino grunted and snorted at him and tried to climb the tank, but failed to get a grip on the smooth-painted staves. So he stood guard abaft the house, looking up.

"There were two other roads to the deck—the port and starboard mizzen rigging, I still had in mind that rifle of the skipper's, and as the second mate, a young fellow just out of the forecastle, made no objections, I slid down the after-swifter of the port rigging and got into the cabin before the skipper or the rhino noticed me.

"I found the cabin flooded, and waded waist-deep to the skipper's room, where I found his Winchester hanging to the bulkhead. Making sure that the magazine was full, I scrambled to the forward companion, where there was a window that gave me a good view of the deck. The skipper was calling the men on the main to come down by the maintopmast stay to the top of the house, and to those on the fore to come down by the backstays to the rail, and then to jump to the water-tanks; and the men were coming down, one by one, even though the rigging swarmed with big monkeys and the corners and hollow spots possibly held poisonous snakes.

"A yell from the mizzen called my attention to one of these, a big fellow of four feet in length whom the skipper had frightened out of his hiding-place on the fife-rail, and he was climbing the mizzen-stay. He rested about six feet up, but completely blocked this path to the deck for the men in the mizzen. However, when I had cleared the deck of the rhino, they could come down my way. I cocked the gun, took careful aim at the big brute's left eye, and let go.

"I missed the eye, but attracted his attention, and he came charging aft through the water. I ducked, knowing that he couldn't climb the flimsy steps to the short length of poop forward of the house without breaking them down with his weight, and, after a moment, peeped out.

"He was just turning to go forward, and, as I knew that a Winchester bullet wouldn't puncture his hide, I saved my shots.

"Meanwhile, all hands but the boys in the mizzen-crosstrees had gained the forward house and were clearing away the two boats, lashed in their chocks, right side up—one to starboard, the other to port. I could see the work going on—saw them smash the skylight over the galley for a man to go down to pass up grub, and saw a man dive down.

"Then I saw another fellow take a beaker from the starboard boat, and, watching his chance when the rhino wasn't looking, drop over and into the starboard forecastle, to fill it from the water-barrel. He passed it up and also the bread-barge. There was some of the cabin stores in the galley, and these they secured easily through the skylight; but I noticed they packed it all in the starboard-boat, though they had cleared away the other.

"I knew I had just fifteen shots in that rifle; but I hadn't looked for further ammunition, and I thought that fifteen would finish the rhino, somehow; so, when the boys above shinned down and joined me, I neglected to ask them to hunt for more, but just peppered away when I thought I saw a good chance, but never hit the one vulnerable spot.

"The second mate wanted to try it, but I wouldn't resign the gun to him. In extreme emergencies, you know, an officer loses his superiority; he becomes a mere man, like the rest. Every time I tickled the brute with a bullet he would come charging aft, but never stopped still when within easy range. Not seeing anyone, he would wheel and go back to his duty at the forward house. To tell the truth, I was a little nervous lest he should be able to mount the poop and get at us.

"The old hippo was happy, swimming and snorting round in the water; and the rhino seemed to have forgotten his grudge, busying himself with his real enemies, human beings. There were about sixteen of these on the forward house, and I noticed that they had ceased the work of stocking the boat, and judged that there was no more grub forward.

"'I say, cap'n,' I called out, 'put some grub and water in the other boat. One boat won't hold us all.'

"'You go to the dickens!' he answered. 'What are you doing in my cabin? Didn't I tell you to keep out of it?'

"'Go yourself!' I yelled. Then I said to the men with me: 'Raid the steward's storeroom and fill your pockets with what you can find. Pack the inside of your shirts.'

"They could find nothing eatable except soda biscuits, and they cleaned out the locker. But there was no water aft.

"Meanwhile the bark was getting lower and lower, and the rhino, to escape the wash, had drifted farther forward. I had wasted twelve bullets by this time, and had but three left. It was best, of course, to kill him before the bark foundered, so that we could get into that port boat and induce the rest to pass over some grub and water. But this was not to be.

"I killed him, all right, but only after we had rushed out at the death flurry of the old craft, floundered forward, seizing handspikes from the racks on the way, and gained the vicinity of the house. Here that murder-minded rhino met us, and I jammed the muzzle into one eye.

"The bullet touched some part of his brain, for he sagged down and grew quiet. And while we mounted the house, the asses and zebras were hee-hawing, the wolf was barking, and the mad elephant, waving his trunk up through the hatch, was trumpeting like a high-pressure exhaust.

"We were just in time. The others had got into the starboard boat, and we bundled into the port. There was no time for a decent launching over the rail, but there was time to sing out for grub and water. The skipper and mate consigned us to the infernal regions.

"'There's not enough to go round,' he declared. 'Take your chance. It's better that part should starve than all.'

"I still had the gun, and had there been time I could have coerced them; but there was no time. In a minute the water had reached the top of the house.

"Then, as the boats floated in the creamy turmoil, we pushed with the oars, and, though half swamped, managed to clear the fore-braces as they went under. There was a mighty roaring of water, and a mighty suction, but the two boats floated, though half full.

"Then we saw that blooming old hippo rise out of the depths and head for us. We shipped the oars and pulled like mad, but we'd gone a quarter of a mile through that heavy sea before we dropped him.

"We couldn't have helped him; he'd have swamped us in a jiffy if he'd got his nose and forepaws over the gunwale. We chewed dry soda biscuits for three days, and were then picked up."

"But the others, Sam?" I asked. "Were they picked up?"

"No," answered Sam with a perceptible quaver in his voice. "They were not. The wolf, the zebras, and the asses could swim, and so could the monkeys, and snakes, after a fashion.

"I don't know what trouble they may or may not have had with these. What I did see, though, as I pulled stroke oar in the race with the hippo, was the big head of the elephant showing occasionally as we rode over the crest of a wave.

"He was waving his trunk in the air, and making for the other boat. They were pulling as hard as we were, but to less avail. They were overladen with men and grub. Each lift of a sea showed them nearer together.

"Then we sank into a hollow.

"When we came up I saw nothing but that waving trunk."

THE FINISHING TOUCH

I

HE WAS BORN WITH A nature as simple and primitive as the physical conditions surrounding him, and endowed with a body so frail and delicate that he barely survived these conditions—which were of frost, and snow, and ice, with winter hurricanes straight from Greenland and summer fogs fed by the Gulf Stream to breed pneumonia and kindred diseases into stronger lungs than his.

But he survived to reach the age of eighteen, a tall, flat-chested, weak-witted butt of the local school, who, while able to struggle along with the ordinary studies at the foot of the class, was yet so poorly endowed with the mathematical sense that he could only master the first four rules of arithmetic. Fractions and decimals were unsolvable mysteries to him. His name was Quinbey—first name John, later Jack.

He was of American birth, the only son of a fisherman, who had taken his smack to an isolated village on the Nova Scotian coast. Here the fisherman did well, and before the boy was half grown owned the finest cottage in the village—which he bought cheap because it was perched on the crest of the hill, exposed to every storm that blew, a nest that none but a sailor could live in. With increasing prosperity he installed a big base-burner, good for the anæmic boy, but bad for himself.

The boy rid himself of coughs and colds; but the father, changing from the chill and the wet of fishing to the warmth and ease of home life, contracted pneumonia and died, leaving the boy in possession of the house and the smack, but not enough ready money to last for a month.

Young Quinbey closed up the house, took in a partner with money, and went fishing for a season, at the end of which the partner—a shrewd business man—owned the smack.

The boy acquired a wonderful increase of health and strength, and a consuming love for a pretty girl of the village, a trader's daughter named Minnie, who repulsed him firmly and emphatically because of his poverty—for the house and base-burner were not desirable assets—and because of his weak mental and physical equipment.

But there is a school for weak mentality and physique—the Seven Seas. And to this school went John Quinbey, first, however, putting in one season on the Georges Bank, where, in a lucky craft, he made money. Richer than ever before in his life, he returned home, to try again for the heart and hand of Minnie, but found her married to the minister, a man as weak, flat-chested, and anæmic as he himself had been.

He reasoned crudely. He did not meet Minnie, but took stock and measure of the minister, a gentleman named Simpson; then, feeling his own expanding chest and enlarging muscles, decided that Minnie would soon be a widow, and he a strong man with money; for he could work, and, having no vices, could save. So, for love of Minnie, he went back to sea, resolved to become a captain, resolved to save every cent he earned, and resolved to balk at no hardship that would lead him to success.

At Boston, he shipped before the mast as able seaman in a big deep-water ship. He was not an able seaman, nor did he become one on this voyage; it required several; but each one marked a steady advance in muscular strength, mental activity, and bank account; and, at the end of the fifth, he signed as boatswain—an able man who knew his work.

He was strong, broad-shouldered, and active; the slightly vacant look in his face that had come from his boyhood incapacity had changed to a frank stare that demanded consideration and respect. He seldom asked a question twice now—once was usually enough. He had a fist that could smash the panels of a door, a voice that he could not modulate to conversational tones—so used was he to sending it against the wind. He did not use tobacco, nor did he drink, for these things cost money, and he was thinking of Minnie, most precious of all things in the world.

At the end of each voyage he visited home, deposited the money he had brought, and waited in the street just long enough for a sight of Minnie, sweet and matronly, and for a sight of the minister, who was holding on to life with a remarkable tenacity. Then he would work his way to Boston, and sign again.

Soon he became a second mate, but never a first, nor a captain. His limitations in arithmetic prevented him from mastering navigation, a necessary acquirement in a first mate or a skipper, and he remained in the position he had reached, close to the sailors, but not of them; sharing their hardships and hard work—for with every reefing or furling match a second mate must go aloft with the men—standing watch with them, washing down decks with them, getting drenched to the skin as often as they, and differing from them only in increase of pay, cabin food, and a dryer bed to sleep in.

But the dryer bed preserved him from the rheumatism and pulmonary troubles that kill all sailors who do not drown, the better food preserved his now iron physique, and the increased pay went into the bank at home.

And so it continued until he was forty years old, when he went home to find Minnie a widow with a grown-up son—a fat, weak-chinned, pale-faced parody on manhood, who never had done a day's work in his life—a "mamma's boy," who was destined for the ministry.

The dark, seamy-faced man of storm and strength, of stress and strain, asked her again to be his wife. He asked her as he would have asked a sailor to sign articles; and the frightened little woman accepted in about the same spirit that would have influenced the sailor; but she made one condition—that he would educate her son for the ministry.

He agreed. Her husband had left her almost nothing, while Quinbey had about ten thousand dollars in the bank. From this he drew the expense of a four years' course at Andover; and, taking the youth to this famous theological college, arranged for his stay there in such a manner as would insure his completing the course—that is, he paid to the president for everything in advance, including, beside tuition and board, a moderate amount of spending money, and traveling expense home and back in vacation.

Then, with Sammy Simpson off his mind for four years at least, Quinbey returned, and married the woman he loved, feeling that he had now earned happiness and the right to remain on land—and smoke.

But he was not born for happiness, and did not recognize it when it came to him. He opened up his house on the hill, fired up the base-burner, and the two sat around it for a month trying to assimilate each other; but they could not. He knew nothing of women; she nothing of such men as him. He never smiled; and, when he joked, the joke was lost in the rumble and grumble of his voice. He caressed her with the gentleness of a grizzly fondling the hunter, and was nonplussed and set back when she cried out in pain.

Afraid of him at first, she soon realized that he knew no better, and responded with the weapons of woman. The man, inured to cold and pain and fatigue, yet was sensitive as a child when it came to his feelings. When she learned this, she kept his nerves quivering with quiet smiles, soft and sarcastic little speeches, and deadening silences, the meaning of which did not strike him at the time because of his transparent frankness and honesty.

He became afraid of her; and she, following up her advantage, wheedled him out of money for clothes, which, though he could not see the need of them, he cheerfully gave her. He loved her devotedly; and, though he never smiled, yet he never frowned, nor spoke a harsh word to her.

But she thought him harsh, and, justified by the thought, continued the marital loot until she grew brave enough to demand a gold watch for Sammy's birthday.

This was not in his program, and he told her so. Then followed a lecture on the duties and shortcomings of fathers, which lasted an hour, and left him shaking like a sick man, sprawled out in the big chair by the fire, and smoking like a high-pressure tug. But she had brought him around, and he had arisen to go out to the town's one jeweler, when she lost all she had won.

"Where are you going?" she asked sharply, as he put on his hat.

"Going out, Minnie," he said, in his jokeless voice, "to get some catnip for you."

He meant it good-humoredly; but it was taken otherwise. The jeweler had no gold watches; but, after a two hours' search, he dug up a wholesaler's catalogue, and, with this in his pocket, Quinbey returned to have Minnie select a watch from it; but she, her trunks, and her belongings were gone, while a note on the table apprised him that she would live with no man who called her a cat.

Troubled in mind, he followed her to the home of her parents, but he was not admitted—nor given a chance to show her the catalogue.

He slept on the problem, and in the morning resolved that a little absence would be good for her; so, as the season had opened, he packed his bag and went out on a fishing trip with friends of his, expecting to be back in a month. It was eight years later when he returned.

His adventures during those eight years can only be summarized. The fishing schooner was cut down by a big ship out of Halifax bound around the Horn; and Quinbey alone of her crew succeeded in springing to her martingale-stay as the smaller craft went under. No one else was saved, though the ship hove to and put out boats to search. Then the ship went on, and, as she met no inbound craft, Quinbey was forced to go with her.

But she did not round Cape Horn. A strong current threw her onto the Patagonian coast near Cape Virgins in a dead calm, and a sudden gale of wind and heavy sea ground her to pieces.

Only John Quinbey was a swimmer of sufficient strength to reach the beach, and here he lay, half dead, for a day, when he arose and struck inland, knowing that Punta Arenas was about a hundred and fifty miles along the coast of the Magellan Strait, and hoping to reach it.

He did not at once. The giant savages of this region caught him and made him one of them, preventing his escape. He was accustomed to hardship, and lived their life, tormented only by the thought that the money at home was deposited in his name, and that he had made no provision whereby the foolish little wife could draw from the bank.

But he still hoped to escape; and, as the tribe drifted inland, he was allowed more liberty. He never abused it, waiting for a final dash, always returning from a jaunt in reasonable time, and earning the confidence of his captors.

When over seven years had passed, he found, in the foothills of the Latorre Mountains, a large, heavy lump of dark metal, which he scraped with his knife and recognized as gold. It was fully the size of a draw bucket, but of what value he could not determine, except that it represented a fortune.

Strong man though he was, he could not carry it a hundred yards without resting, yet he carried it, not back to the tribe, but in a southwesterly direction, toward Punta Arenas. When forced to return, he hid it, taking careful bearings, and rejoined his masters. He waited a few days before the next trip, then moved it a few miles farther on.

In this way, exciting no suspicion, he shifted his find, step by step, until he had it on a well-defined trail that could lead nowhere but to the lonely port he was making for. Then, after a few days' rest, he packed a bundle of dried meat, took with him a native-made rope by which to drag the heavy nugget, and left the camp in the dark of night.

He reached his treasure by daylight, and started along the trail. He was not pursued, and ten days later, half starved, half mad, his shoulders bleeding from the chafe of the rope, and every bone in his body aching with the pain of fatigue, he dragged his burden onto a rickety wharf at Punta Arenas where an eastbound steamer was coaling. Her captain was an honest man. He took Quinbey on board, took him to Boston, and helped him turn the nugget into cash—fifty thousand dollars. Then Quinbey went home.

II

QUINBEY HAD BEEN RIGHT ABOUT the money in the bank. It was a tidy sum to retain on deposit, and the bank officials had heartlessly refused to pay any of it out to Mrs. Quinbey. She did not attempt to draw until her sulks left her, which occurred after the jeweler, intent upon the sale of a watch, had called upon her, and when the villagers had informed her that Quinbey had gone fishing. Then, disappointed, and somewhat worried over the future, she returned to the house on the hill, and, as it was still cold, lit up the big base-burner from the scanty stock of coal.

As the weeks grew into months and the fishing schooner did not return, she did not, like the rest of the villagers, give her husband up as lost—rather, she believed him alive, hoped for his return, and revised her opinion of him.

Soon—yet long before the grocer, the butcher, and the coal man had refused further credit—she realized that she loved the crude man she had known but a month, but who had loved her for twenty years; and, with tears streaming down her face, she prayed for his safety and return with more fervency than for the beloved son at Andover. This person wrote filial letters home, assuring her of protection and support when he returned; but they brought her small comfort, for the time was at hand when she must pay cash or go without the necessities of life.

Then Sammy came home on his first vacation, and, learning of the money in the bank, used his prestige and address to such advantage that he persuaded the local authorities to declare Quinbey legally dead—an easy matter on that coast of many wrecks.

Righteously indignant at the selfishness of the bank officials, he induced his mother to withdraw the money—shrunk to eight thousand dollars—from the bank, and allow him to take it to Boston, where, in a larger and safer bank, it would draw interest, and on which she could write checks in payment of her bills.

She consented, and Sammy departed with the money. But at Boston, before reaching the bank, he traversed the highways and the byways of the big city, imbibed certain and sundry liquids known to him only by name, loved his fellow men, and met fellow men of like state of mind, who, seeing a stranger, took him in.

He was stripped to empty pockets, spent a night in a cell, and only by the help of another clergyman was he shipped back to Andover with a letter to the president.

From here he wrote to his mother a garbled account of his adventures; and, as the president of the college mercifully forbore writing her the truth, the poor woman merely wept a little, prayed a little, and took up her burden.

Her parents were old and indigent, unable to more than house her for a few days at a time. As minister's wife, she had made no friends that would help her now in a way befitting her position. As for herself, with only a village education, she could not even teach, even though able to found a school.

But every mother and daughter, sister and grand-ma'am in the village was willing to give her work by the day for the mere pleasure of gloating; and at this work she went bravely.

The sneers and insults she received soon limited her journeyings from home, and she finally became the village wash-woman. The kitchen of the house was turned into a laundry, and the big base-burner allowed to grow cold; for she could not afford two fires.

In her laundry she worked, and in wintertime slept, and only on Saturdays was she seen on the street, when, with deepening lines in her face and a growing gray tinge to her hair, she struggled back and forth with her basket of clothes. But she earned her living, and looked forward hopefully to the return of her husband and assuredly to the return of her son, who would care for her.

Sammy only came home on the first vacation; the next three he spent at the homes of classmates. But at last the four years' course was ended, and, with nowhere else to go, he appeared, an ordained minister of the Gospel, but unattached.

The Reverend Samuel Simpson, as we must know him now, was twenty-four years old, as pale as ever, fatter than ever, with a chin that, because of the fat, seemed to recede still farther into his neck. His mother rejoiced over him, was proud of him, and believed that her troubles were now ended.

The villagers welcomed him, and the gray old pastor of the church once presided over by his father invited him to preach. He did so, delivering his one sermon; but the delivery and the sermon were not of a character that would inspire the congregation to empty the pulpit for him, so the young preacher went home to wait, as Quinbey had waited, for that pulpit to become vacant by death.

But he deplored the coldness of the house, and ordered coal on credit for the base-burner; also he deplored the hard labor of his mother, assured her that the necessity for it would soon end, but did nothing himself toward this end; for, in truth, there was nothing he could do but preach; and the gray old pastor seemed as tenacious of life as his own father had been.

The mother was content, however, except for the always present, but lessening, hope that her husband would return, and happy in the company of her educated and accomplished son. And so, as bravely as ever, she carried her burden through the streets, not only on Saturdays now, but on Wednesdays, because, with another mouth to feed, she must of needs wash more clothes.

And so the time went on, the Reverend Samuel Simpson growing seedier of raiment and fatter of body, enduring patiently the sneers and sarcasms of the indignant men of the village, while the mother's face grew thinner, her body weaker, and her once blond hair so gray that she looked ten years beyond her age. Then, four years after the son's return, the breaking point came. With the front of her garments dripping wet, she stood erect from her tub, looked at him where he sat near the kitchen fire—the base-burner had long been cold—and said:

"Sammy, you must go to work. I can do no more. It is killing me."

"But what can I do, mother dear?" he answered kindly.

"I do not know," she said wearily. "Something, maybe, that will help. You are educated. You might write for the Boston papers, or the magazines. Or you might find a pulpit somewhere else, and send me some money once in a while."

"What, and leave you alone, mother? Not for the world would I desert you. You are my mother, and have cared for me. But I have thought of writing. I have been thinking for years of a literary career, only I have not been able to decide which branch of literature I am best fitted for."

"Well, Sammy," said the mother, as she bent over her tub, "I cannot decide for you; but something must be done."

"And I will do it, mother," he shouted loudly—so loudly that neither heard the opening of the front door, nor the sound of heavy footsteps coming toward the kitchen.

Then a big, dark-faced man, with hair as gray as her own, seized her around the waist, lifted her into his arms, and rained kisses on her face and lips while she screamed, then, as she recognized him, fainted away. Still holding her, he lifted his foot, exerted a slight effort of strength, and pushed the tubful of suds and clothes off its base, upsetting it squarely over the head of the Reverend Samuel Simpson, who nearly choked before getting himself clear.

"I've been hearing things about you down at the store," said Quinbey, "and I'll 'tend to your case directly."

Then he carried the limp little woman into the bedroom, stripped off her wet garments, and covered her warmly, while he kissed her back to consciousness.

"Oh, John," she said, when she could speak, "I knew you'd come back, but, oh, the long waiting! I've been punished, John, punished bitterly."

"There'll be no more of it, Minnie," he said. "I've come home rich— that is, rich for this town. Your work is ended. They told me at the store about your son loafing on you all these years while you took in washing. But how about the money in the bank? Couldn't you get it?"

"Oh, yes, John," she answered simply. "But Sammy took it to Boston to deposit, and was robbed of it."

"Um-hum-m-m," grunted Quinbey. "The savings of twenty years at sea!" Briefly she recounted Sammy's story of the wrong done him; but he made no comment beyond saying that he would look into it.

"He's got to go to work," he added grimly. "I don't know what he can do except preach, and perhaps he can't do that. I'll write to Andover and get his record. But how about the house? It's cold. Out of coal?"

"We've got very little, John. We couldn't afford two fires."

Quinbey left her, and found his stepson in his room, changing his wet clothing for dry.

"Take this money," he said, handing him a bill, "and go down to the coal dock. Order a ton up here at once."

"I will, sir," answered Sammy, with dignity, "when I've recovered somewhat from your extremely brutal treatment of me. I must be dry before I go out on this cold day."

But he went out, shirtless and coatless, at the end of Quinbey's arm; and, as it really was cold, he hurried on his errand, and returned. Before long the base-burner was roaring, and Quinbey was recounting his adventures to his happy-faced wife; while Sammy, in the kitchen, finished up the wash. Later on he delivered it; but no more washing of other folks' clothing was ever done in that house.

Quinbey wrote to Andover, and in a few days received a reply, which he read to his wife. It was a true account of Sammy's mishap in Boston; and, while Quinbey grinned—he could not smile—the mother wept silently, but asked no forgiveness for her wayward son. And when he rummaged a bureau, and brought forth an old jeweler's catalogue, asking her to choose a watch for Sammy, she felt that it was granted; but she did not yet know Quinbey.

Sammy wore the watch proudly; and for the rest of the cold weather the three sat about the base-burner, while the color came back to the little woman's face, and self-confidence to the shaken mind of Sammy. He actually began to like his rough stepfather; and only an outsider might have guessed, by the somber light in Quinbey's dark eyes when they rested upon him, that he did not like his stepson.

In the spring, as soon as the frost and snow were gone, Quinbey employed laborers to flatten the ground near his house to the extent of a hundred feet by ten; then, with stakes, he laid out the plan of a ship's deck. Next he contracted with spar makers, ship carpenters, and ship chandlers for material and labor; and before June three masts were erected, each with topmast, top-gallant, and royal mast, the standing rigging of which was set up to strong posts driven into the ground; then followed yards, canvas, and running gear, and soon a complete ship of small dimensions, but without a hull, adorned the crest of the hill.

As Quinbey explained to the questioning villagers, he would go to sea no more, but, having spent his life at sea, wanted a reminder—something to look at—a plaything.

Sammy was an interested spectator of the work, and Quinbey was kind to him, answering his questions, and even betraying some solicitude that he should understand the rig of a ship, the names of the ropes and sails, and the manner of handling them. He even went so far as to hire a couple of sailors to climb aloft, to loose and furl canvas, again and again, until Sammy understood.

Then the cold weather came on, and the base-burner was lit; and with the cold weather came the snow, and the icy sleet, and the hurricane gales from Greenland, striking the crest of that hill with a force that threatened to tear the dummy ship from the ground. And on particularly stormy nights, the villagers, snug in their warm beds, would waken for a moment at a sound louder than the gale—the sound of Quinbey's voice, which, in a calm, would carry a mile. And the voice would cry:

"All hands on deck to make sail. Out wi' you, you blasted lubber, and lay aloft. Up wi' you, and loose that mainsail, and, when you've got it loose, furl it. I'll show you how I earned that money. Up wi' you, 'fore I give you a rope's end."

And sometimes, in the lulls, they could hear Sammy's shrieks of pain, and the thwack of the rope's end.

The Rock

"I tell ye I saw it—wi' these eyes I saw it!"

"You think you seen it."

"Now I quit. Ye talk like every mate or skipper or Consul I've told this to. Just the same, I never git to the end o' the third day out, either way,—I'm in a six-day boat, ye know—but what the nervousness gits me, an' I'm no good for twelve hours, until I know we're past the spot."

"A rock, you say, in the middle o' the Atlantic? Why isn't it known and charted?"

"Because it's awash an' visible only at the fall o' the spring tides."

"How is it that no one else saw it but you?"

"I was the only man aloft. She was a hemp-rigged old ballyhoo out o' Quebec, an' gear was chafin' through all the time. I was passin' a new seizin' on the collar o' the foretopmast stay, when I squinted ahead through the fog, and there it was black an' shiny, an' murderous, about forty feet long, I should judge, and five feet or so out o' water, right dead under the bow. I could see the lift o' the water where the current pushed ag'in' it, and the swirl on t'other side, showin' it was no derelict, bottom up. No, it was a rock. 'Starboard!' I yells to the felly at the wheel. 'Starboard! Hard up!' Well, the skipper was below, an' the second mate, who had the deck, was mixin' paint under the fo'c'sle; so the wheel went up an' the old wagon payed off 'fore the wind. Then I lost it myself in the fog, an', as I couldn't point out anything to the skipper when he come up, I was called down an' damned for a fool. But I saw it, just the same, a big rock halfway across, and squarely between the lane routes!"

"How do you know that?"

"The skipper wasn't above givin' me the ship's position—forty-seven north; thirty-seven twenty west. That's between the lanes, an' I'll bet the *Narconic* is at the base o' that rock, to say nothin' o' the *Pacific*, the *President*, and t'others."

The wabbly little West Street horse car had reached the White Star dock by this and the two men stepped off. Steamship sailors, I knew. I had never seen them before, and have never seen them since; but their conversation produced a marked impression upon me, and I could not shake off a feeling—not of itself a remembrance, however—that I had heard something of the kind before. A submerged rock in mid-Atlantic. But it was incredible, and at last I put it from my mind as a "galley yarn."

But next morning it was back, in company with another galley yarn, one I barely remembered as having heard ten years before from an old Confederate man-o'-war'sman who had sailed with Semmes in the *Alabama*. The yarn pertained to the pursuit of a Northern merchant ship, and I give only the conclusion.

"We were gaining fast," he had said, "and hoped to bring her to before breakfast; for at daylight she was but three miles or so ahead, every sail drawing and every detail of spar, canvas, and hull showing clear in the morning light. And then, while we looked at her, she quickly settled under, not head first or stern first, as is usual, but on an even keel. They had no time to start a brace or a halyard; there was not time for her to answer to her wheel, if it had been shifted. She just went down as though something had hooked onto her keel and dragged her under. I never learned her name; but she must have been bound out of New York or Boston, for some French port in the Channel. We picked up one of her men, a Dago who couldn't tell her name, and only this much as to what happened. A ripping, crashing sound began forward and worked its way aft, ending at the stern, and we could only surmise that something—a submerged derelict, perhaps—had scraped the bottom out of her."

Memory is treacherous. In a few days I had forgotten this yarn with the other, and might never have recalled it had I not ascended to an upper floor in the lofty Flatiron Building, and looked out of a window at the loftier, but unfinished, tower of the Metropolitan Building across the park. It was a damp, dismal day of fog; but at my elevation I could see clear of it. I was above it, looking over an undulating sea of cloud bank from which the tower rose, massive and mighty, apparently floating on end, like an immense spar buoy at the turn of the tide. The rest of New York lay hidden beneath that silent gray ocean of fog.

Interesting as it was of itself, it was not the spectacle before me that gripped and held me, but an associated idea. As it was the first time I had ever seen a skyscraper lift itself above the clouds, so it naturally reminded me of the first time I had seen a mountaintop above the clouds. This was Krakatoa Island, a conical mountain rising from the sea in the Straits of Sunda, but since submerged in the Java earthquake.

With this mental picture before me, my thoughts touched upon other happenings of that boyhood voyage—the long, tedious beat through the straits against light head winds and a continuous head tide; the man-killing log windlass, round which we hove, and lightened, chain of an eight-inch link; the natives, with their welcome fruit in exchange for trinkets; and, lastly, the white-haired old pilot, who came forward to visit me one evening on anchor watch.

And then, like an inspired flash, there surged into my mind, not only the two galley yarns, but the story told by the pilot—a story of such burning power and horror that, though forgotten for a generation, it spelled itself out, word for word, as I stared into the fog from the window, exactly as the old man had told it.

He had heard from the skipper that I was from the same part of New York State as himself, and he had come forward for news of home. I could give him little. I knew no one that he knew; the small town that give him birth was not far from my own, but was only a name to me. Still he remained to talk. My up-State accent pleased him, he said, and reminded him of home, which he had not seen for forty years, and which he hardly hoped to see. He was sixty-five; two shocks had come, and the third would finish him.

"But I'm an old, experienced man, my boy," he said, "and I can give you my life's wisdom in three short rules, easy to remember and easy to follow. Stick to your skipper; leave liquor alone; and never, under any provocation, engage in mutiny. I broke every one of these, and here I've been, for half a lifetime, an exile, afraid to go home."

Not realizing how sorely I needed this wisdom, but keenly interested in mutiny, piracy, and such fancies of boyhood, I asked for light, and he gave it to me.

"I won't tell you the name of the ship," he said; "for you'll be a boy for some time to come, and you might talk about it. Nor will I give you the real names of the men engaged in that mutiny; for it is only forty years back, and there may be men alive yet who will be interested in the fate of the ship; though none, I expect, who would care much about her crew. But I'll tell you that her crew was the toughest gang I ever saw in a forecastle, and her skipper and mate the most inhuman brutes I ever saw aft. I was second mate, and, having won my berth in deep water, thought I was something of a bucko; but I found my masters there. The ship, I may as well say, was one of the packets that traded between New York and Liverpool, sometimes carrying passengers, but not always. We had none this trip.

"Before we were two days out from Sandy Hook I got a taste of the skipper's caliber. A man aloft—a big, red-headed fellow, gave me an insolent answer from the cro'-jack yard, and I called him down. When he reached the deck I was ready, and sent him reeling over the break of the poop with one smash on the jaw. He was satisfied to go aloft again and answer civilly when spoken to; but the skipper, who had watched the performance, was not. He called me over to the lee alley and faced me, his face fairly alive with rage and contempt.

"'Say, you—you—you Sunday school teacher! Is that the way you expect to handle men in these packets? Hey?'

"'I didn't hit him hard, sir,' I answered. 'I didn't hurt him. He's aloft now, at work.'

"'You didn't hurt him? No, I'll warrant you didn't! Why didn't you follow him up, watch for his knife, and take it away from him? 'Fraid of him? Hey? How do you expect to get along wi' this kind of a crew if you're content with one smash? Follow it up, man! Follow up your first blow with another, and another, till you're sure of him.'

"'Oh, I understand, Captain,' I said. 'Well, sir, I'm not worrying over any further trouble with that fellow. He's had enough.'

"'Make sure of it. You'll get no sympathy from me if he wins out.'

"It seems that the way of deep water was not the way of the packets. Somewhat impressed by this, I waited until eight bells, when the red-head came down—his job was merely the passing of new ribbons in place of old—and tackled him amidships, as he went forward.

"'Well,' I said. 'What do you think? The skipper says I didn't give you enough. Have you had enough, or do you want more?'

"He looked me squarely in the eyes, and his hand wandered toward his sheath knife in his belt. Mine wandered toward a pistol in my hip pocket.

"'I'm 'fore the mast, sir,' he said; 'and as a man 'fore the mast—yes, of course I've had enough. But I've been aft, and I may be aft again. Then, too, you may be 'fore the mast. Well, sir, I know the law.'

"'Forecastle lawyer, are you?' I asked derisively.

"'Yes, and more,' he exploded. 'Your superior in seamanship, you blanked whitewashed son of a ship owner!'

"My fist shot out; but he dodged it, and ran forward. I sent a belaying pin after him, and it hit him on the shoulder; but I doubt that it hurt him.

"In the next twenty-four hours four men came aft to the skipper for medical treatment from the medicine chest. Red-head had disabled them, in one way or another. One had a broken rib, the result of a punch; the skipper set it. Another had lost some teeth, and showed a few more that were loose. The skipper called upon the carpenter and his pliers to remove these, and sent the man forward. Another was carried aft, unconscious from a fist blow under the ear; and the skipper could only lay him out on a cabin transom to wait until he came to. The last was a case of asthma. Red-head had planted his fist plumb upon his throat, and the resultant inflammation threatened to strangle the man. But the skipper gave him a porous plaster for his chest, and a big cathartic pill by means of which the man came around. You know the Yankee skipper's formula: break your leg or lose your mother—take a pill.

"Well, the outcome of this was that the skipper held a conference of himself, the first mate, and myself. He stated the situation: a man forward was a menace to the tranquillity and the safety of the ship. Who would take him down?

"The first mate, with a look of patronizing pity at me, said to the captain, 'I'll do this, if nobody else can,' again the look of pity. 'I'll show him who's who, and what, and which.'

"'Well,' said the skipper, 'do so, or I'll be afraid of my officers.'

"I looked on while the mate called that troublesome malcontent down from aloft, where he had reported the paral seizing of the fore royal yard adrift without saying sir to Mr. Parker. I watched tranquilly, while the big, whiskered first mate, meeting the man as he dropped from the fore-rigging to the deck, received a threshing of fists and kicks that laid him out. We carried him aft, while Red-head retired to the forecastle. And, as we nursed the mate back to self-respect, we heard the profane vows of Red-head to clean us up, all of us.

"The skipper was furious. 'Have I got to go forrard and lick that fellow?' he said. 'Haven't I got a mate aft able to do his duty?'

"'Why not put him in irons, captain?' I asked. 'I knocked him off the poop once, and made him run next time. That seems to be enough as far as I'm concerned.'

"The skipper glared at me. 'And do you think,' he said sneeringly, 'that he ran because he was afraid of you? He's afraid of the irons and of the law. But that's just why we don't appeal to the irons and the law in these packets. It's a point of honor with us; and—yes, a matter of policy. We couldn't get crews after a time if we ironed and jailed 'em for each offense. No, that man must be properly licked, and if you can't do it, I'll have to do it myself.'

"'I can do it,' I answered quietly, and went forward.

"Mike—for that was the name he gave—was in my watch, and should have remained on deck. I found him in the empty starboard forecastle and called him out. He came, with a bad look in his eyes.

"'Put your knife on the water tank alongside my gun,' I said, 'and come aft where there's a clear space. We'll find out who runs this ship, you or the afterguard.'

"'That sounds fair,' he said; 'but how about the after clap? This is not my proposition.'

"'You mean darbies? There'll be none. The skipper wants you licked into shape, so you'll be useful. Come on.'

"We laid our weapons on the tank as we passed it, and faced each other abreast of the main hatch. The skipper looked on from the poop; the carpenter and cook came out of their shops to witness; and of course the watch, working aloft, stopped work to look down on us. The sea was smooth, the wind mild and fair, and the ship slid along with very little pitching or rolling; so it was a fair fight.

"Mike was a game fighter; but I was just a little heavier, just a little more skilled, and had just a little longer reach; so I soon had him going. I backed him completely round the hatch, and when I had him up to windward again, both his eyes were half closed and his nose broken and bleeding. So far I had not been struck, and I decided now to finish him. I put all my strength and the whole weight of my body into that smash, aiming for the point of his chin; but he saw it coming and attempted to duck. My closed fist brought up with a crash on the top of his big bullet head; for he was slow and groggy, and didn't duck low enough. However, it didn't hurt him, while the effect upon me was to break every small bone in my hand. It was like slugging a windlass bitt; for he leaned partly forward, and hardly budged under the blow.

"I could not repress a slight grunt of pain, and I simply had to stop, and rub my sore hand with the other. He saw and heard; then he came for me, and the rest of the fight was the other way. I fought as I could, one-handed, for I couldn't even guard with my right; but it was no use. He soon had me going, and the last I remember of the fight was a sickening smash under the ear. I don't remember hitting the deck; but when I came to my senses I was laid out in the weather scuppers, and the skipper was down off the poop, talking to Mike.

"'So,' the skipper was saying, 'you are Red Macklin, are you? I've heard of you.' I also had heard of him; for Red Macklin's fame was international. He was a bullying, murderous scoundrel who had perhaps killed more sailors than any other first mate on the western ocean, and who, about five years previous, had foolishly shot his captain. To kill a sailor is one thing, to shoot a skipper is another.

"'Yes, sir,' answered Mike respectfully. 'I've just finished my time for that gun play on Captain Blaine, and am not likely to repeat it. But my prospects were done for, and I had to ship 'fore the mast.'

"'You're a navigator, of course. Bring your dunnage into the first mate's room and take his place. Put his dunnage into the second mate's room, and make that duffer in the scuppers bundle his traps into the forecastle. I want no weaklings aft with me.'

"I scrambled to my feet at this; but—Well, there's no use detailing the argument that followed. I had to go forward peaceably or lose my prospects, like Red Macklin. And I had chosen the western ocean trade because of what I thought my fitness for it, and because in these short trips a man can the more quickly attract the notice of an owner. And I understood now why Macklin had run from me when he knew I had a gun; why he had licked his shipmates; and the reason of his studied insolence to Mr. Parker and myself. He knew the ways of the packets, and, while avoiding guns and irons, he sought to attract the skipper's attention to his prowess. I thought it somewhat severe that Mr. Parker, who had put up no kind of a fight, should be kept aft instead of me, until I reflected that Mr. Parker, with two whole fists, might still be good for any man on board except Macklin; while I, with only one, couldn't lick anybody. It was merely the survival of the fittest, and I was not fit.

"However, I drew comfort from the thought that when my hand got well I could win back my berth in the same manner, and to this end applied at once to the captain for bandages and splints from the medicine chest. He responded like a brother; but earned none of my gratitude, for I considered the medicine chest as furnished out of the Marine Hospital dues, which I had paid for years.

"I had noticed that my pistol and Macklin's knife had disappeared from the water tank, and supposed that he, as the first act in his new position, had confiscated them. So, as I had no use for a gun while 'fore the mast, I put the matter from my mind. I meant to sing small, until my hand was well.

"But what followed in that ship shows how little we can depend upon our good resolutions. I was still in the starboard watch, having taken Macklin's place forward, while he, as mate, had charge of the port watch, and Mr. Parker as second, became my watch officer. So far there had been no friction between Mr. Parker and myself; but now I found the man dead down on me, as though he blamed me for his licking and his change of office.

"One-handed, I was almost useless around decks, and could not steer except in the finest of weather; but this made no difference. I was hounded, cursed, and struck, not only by Parker, but by the skipper and Macklin. Some kind of armed neutrality must have sprung up between Macklin and Parker with regard to me; but I could only ascribe the skipper's new personal attitude to a distrust of my philosophy, which, while impelling me to make the best of matters, may have seemed to him the calm before the storm. I escaped Macklin's abuse, however, except in the dog watches, when all hands were on deck.

"They damned, deviled, and degraded me, keeping me all night on lookout, and rousing me from sleep at any time of the day watch below to climb aloft and loose a royal stop buntlines, or remove an Irish pennant—a loose rope yarn, you know—from any part of the rigging. My nerves went back on me from loss of sleep and futile anger and brooding; and once, when Macklin stripped off the sling I had rigged to hold my sore fist, and knocked me down for protesting, I saw red for a moment.

"Even so, nothing might have happened—had not the crew been included in the drill they were serving me. As an old hand in deep-water ships, I knew the absolute necessity of preserving discipline, and that this can be done only by occasionally knocking down a malcontent; but no such considerations demanded the wholesale clubbing with heavers and handspikes which the men got from the trio. Belaying pins were not used—they were too small and light for the gentlemen. Macklin had four deadly enemies when he went aft, and soon every man forward had a grievance, and voiced it in muttered profanity that held many a threat of death. I fancy that it was my presence in the forecastle that inspired all this ill treatment; no doubt I was regarded as a bad example, whose influence over the men must be offset by stern, repressive measures, but whom they would not remove because of their dislike of the law. For the law could reach a skipper or mate, as Macklin well knew.

"And the crew? Never was a wild, half-crazy herd of Liverpool Irishmen kept under control as that crowd was by a bad example. While aft I had treated them well, and they liked me for my scrap with Macklin; so, they listened while I counseled submission and avoidance of legal consequences—which last was the only point I made. They feared neither man, God, nor devil; but they did fear the law, and grew quiet when I talked of jail and the gallows. And this fear possibly accounted for my finding my pistol—a newly invented Colt revolver— lying in my bunk, one morning when I came in from a long night's lookout to get my breakfast.

"'Who put this here?' I demanded. 'Who had my gun?'

"No one would acknowledge the gift; but the state of mind behind it was given in the remark of one, 'Now ye've got it again, use it!'

"I tucked it under my mattress, resolved not to use it; but a little later put it into my trousers pocket. Fear of the law, forward and aft, began to yield to fear of death. Men openly sharpened their knives, and the afterguard ostentatiously showed their pistols. Their pistols were not so good as mine—they were double-barreled, muzzle-loading derringers, with only two shots.

"Things culminated on a moonlight night when we were charging along before a quartering whole sail breeze, making, I should judge, about eleven knots. I was on lookout, as usual, and keeping a good one I know, even though my eyes would half close at times from sheer need of sleep. It was about seven bells of the first watch and for some reason or other—perhaps the strong moonlight, which keeps some people awake—both the skipper and the first mate were on deck, and standing aft near the wheel, while Mr. Parker stood his watch on the poop forward of the after house. The men walked up and down between the fore and main rigging.

"A faint light showed up ahead and to leeward. I opened my eyes wide to make sure, and saw the faint shadowy outlines of hull and canvas—a ship close hauled across our bows. Then I sang out:

"'Light ho! Ship on the port tack two points off the starboard bow, sir!'

"'Light ho, is it?' bellowed the skipper. 'Put another man on lookout and send that scow bunker aft here, Mr. Parker!'

"A man came and relieved me. Wondering what was up now, I went aft, and the skipper and two mates met me at the break of the poop.

"'You get up there to the weather maintopsail yard arm, you — blind-eyed farmer,' snarled the skipper, 'and keep your lookout there! D'ye hear? I saw that light ten minutes before you sang out.'

"'I reported it as soon as I saw it, sir,' I answered civilly.

"'None o' your lip! Get up there! And say—'

"I had answered and turned, in no way bothered by the change. I was to put in the rest of the night on the yard; but I could sit down and rest my bones.

"The skipper modified this. 'You keep your lookout there, and when the bell strikes, you call out, "All's well, weather maintopsail yard arm!" Then you flap your arms like wings, and crow like a rooster, and, you say, "God bless Captain Black, and Mr. Macklin, and Mr. Parker!" D'you hear?'

"'Yes, sir,' I said, and went aloft, boiling over with humiliation and rage. Of what use was life, I thought, and success at sea if it was to be bought at such a price in manhood and self-respect? The more I thought of it the stronger grew my resolve to end it in some way.

"It was the man at the wheel who showed me the way. He was a hot-tempered Irishman, a good seaman; but an indifferent helmsman. He had put the ship off a couple of points at the skipper's order, so as to pass under the stern of the ship ahead, and had some trouble in steadying to the new course. He came in for a round of abuse from the three, and at last was relieved, while the skipper gave him instructions similar to mine. He was to take the lee maintopsail yard, call out the bells when struck on deck, and conclude with the cock-crow and blessing on his lords and masters. I heard his furious curses as he reached the yard and slid out to leeward.

"We passed under the stern of the other ship, and I judged by her rig that she was beating her way west, possibly to New York or Boston. As she dropped out of sight astern, eight bells struck on deck. The lookout on the forecastle called out, 'Eight bells, t'gallant fo'cas'le! All's well!' in the peculiar singsong they have in that trade. I repeated my call from the weather yard arm; but I left out the crow and the prayer for blessings. The skipper and mates were looking up at me, and I saw that the first was about to sing out something; but Casey over to leeward interrupted.

"'Eight bells!' he called. 'See maintopsail yard arm. All's well, an' blankety blank yer black hearts and cowardly sools to damnation, Captain Black, Mister Macklin, an' Mister Parker!'

"'What's that—what?' stuttered the skipper. 'Weather yard arm there! What do *you* say?'

"'Go to hell!' I answered furiously.

"The skipper was near his cabin window, and I saw him reach within. Casey, over to leeward, filled the night with his imprecations. He called down, not blessings, but the tortures of the damned on his tormentors, and attracted the skipper's attention from me. When he stood up he held a short-barreled rifle, and with this he took careful aim at Casey. Then there was a spat of flame, a report, a puff of smoke floating over the house, and Casey, an oath stopped on his lips, sprawled downward into the sea.

"The watch had been called, and appeared in time to see this. I heard the explosive but muttered comments, and then a concerted snarl of hatred and rage as they rushed aft. But I paid no present attention to it. I had drawn my pistol, and was taking careful aim with my left hand at the captain, not so much determined by fear that I should be next as by a resolve, born of my emotions before the shooting, to bring things to an end.

"The skipper looked up at me and got the bullet, fairly in the face, I think, but I never was sure just where I hit him. He dropped, however, and lay still, while the two mates made a dive for the forward companion.

"Macklin got in; but not so Parker. The enraged men caught him just outside the door, slammed in his face by Macklin, and I had one glimpse of him as I scrambled in along the footrope. He was in the center of a circle of flourishing sheath knives, his voice of command nearly silenced by the vengeful shouts and oaths of the men, and when I looked again, as I dropped into the rigging, he was prone on his back, while the men were surging aft to enter the cabin by the after companion. But Macklin was ahead of them, and had bolted it as he had the other.

"I descended and mounted to the poop.

"'Ye'll have to take command, sir,' said a big, red-eyed fellow, named Finnegan. 'Yer the shipped sicond mate, an' it b'langs to ye.'

"'Is the skipper dead?' I asked.

"'Dead, as he ought to be, the murderer! Ye did well, sir!'

"'And Mr. Parker?' I glanced at the quiet, bleeding form at my feet.

"'He's in small pieces, hild togither be his bones.'

"'Not a pleasant prospect for me,' I said; 'but I'm in for it, same as all of us. We'll have to stand trial; for there's no escape. But there's a rat down in his hole that we'll have to catch. Look out, or he'll pot one of you through his window!'

"I spoke at random, yet none too soon. A pistol exploded in the mate's window, and a man went down, shot through the heart—the last one to join the rush over to starboard. But the rush continued to the capstan bar rack amidships, and, armed with these handy clubs, they came back to batter in the companion. Macklin did not fire again, and I was on the point of asking him out, to surrender on terms of amnesty and deposition, when a crashing, grinding jar shook the ship from bow to stern, and all three topgallant masts went out of her, snapping at the caps and falling forward. We had struck a rock in midocean.

"There was no more thought of Macklin. As we jumped to the main deck and ran forward like sheep, the jars and jolts were resumed, working aft, while the ship reeled far over to leeward. Chips was on deck, and I got him to sound the well. 'Four feet, and coming in fast!' he called, and the men rushed for the boats on the forward house, while I went aft to the wheel. I had never heard of a rock in this part of the Atlantic, and thought for a moment that we might have hit a submerged derelict; but soon put that thought away; nothing but solid and jagged rock could so tear into a ship's bottom.

"'No steerage way, sir,' said the man at the wheel. 'She's fallen off due south.'

"'Drop your wheel,' I said, 'and lend a hand with the boats.'

"I waited a few moments before following him, looking around at the prospect. Since I had gone aloft the wind had hauled to the north and died down to a gentle breeze, which barely ruffled the very slight ground swell. It was not the pressure of this wind that had driven the ship over the rock until she hung, pivoted, at a point near the stern; it was the ship's momentum. The wind, however, had swung her head to the south, and it was bringing down on us a cold, damp fog out of the north, which already had shut out the moon and rendered indistinct the forms of the men at work on the boats. I could see, however, that the bow had settled nearly under, and knew that it was only a question of moments when the ship would slide, head first, down the declivity. I ran forward, and just as I started a report rang out from the after companion and a bullet furrowed my hair. I had forgotten Macklin, but had moved just in time.

"Furious with anger and hatred, I halted in the alley and reached for my revolver; but it was gone from my pocket—jolted out, perhaps, as we jumped off the poop. So, I left Macklin to his own problem, and joined the men.

"There were two whaleboats, which we had carried upside down on the forward house, and when I got there I found that the men, sailors all from head to foot, had turned them over, fitted in the bottom plugs, and bent long painters that led forward outside the rigging. There was no time to rig hoisting tackles aloft, nor was there need, as a gang to each could launch them bodily over, one on either side.

"Sailors all, from head to feet, but wild 'packet rats' whose necks were already in their halters! I considered my chance in an open boat with that crowd, and thought of my gun, lying somewhere aft on the main deck. Resolved to risk another shot from Macklin rather than my chance unarmed among the men, I turned back, watching the cabin windows with one eye and searching the deck with the other; but I saw no gun, and perhaps Macklin did not see me, for there was no more shooting.

"Giving it up at last, I ran forward as both boats went over the side and the men were tumbling into them. As I ran I noticed the steeper incline to the deck, and that the forecastle was submerged; but I was not prepared for the sudden launch of the ship into the sea, nor the sickening crash of riven timbers as her after body was torn away, and which drowned my shouts to the men.

"In a roaring, yeasty froth of tumultuous water, I went under, and when I at last came to the surface, half drowned, I was alone on the sea, hidden from the boats by the thick envelope of fog. I shouted, and was answered faintly; but not able to determine the direction the sound came from, I could only shout again and tread water, hoping to make sure.

"But I could not make sure; sound is twisted around amazingly in fog, and little by little the calls grew fainter. I was tired out already, and my useless right arm ached with the hard usage it had lately received. In the next few minutes, while my chin sank lower and lower in the water, I thought of about every incident of my life; but just as the first mouthful went down my throat my right foot hit something, and the next moment I was standing on it—a hard, firm substance which could be nothing but the rock.

"At first I found difficulty in holding my footing until I realized that I must breast a current of about half a knot; but when I had mastered the knack I found no trouble. Feeling carefully with my feet, I explored the ground under foot, and following a rise to where it ended found myself waist high out of water. This was better than nothing, and I resumed my shouts to the men in the boats. At times they answered; but very faintly, and after a while they grew silent. And then, from somewhere out of the fog came the faint stroke of a small bell. I shouted again; but was not answered.

"There was very little wind, and but a perceptible heave of the ground swell; so I was bothered at first only by the dense fog and the current. But after a time I had other troubles, of a mental nature. The water was unquestionably rising, and whether or not it would rise above my chin was an unsolvable problem. I did not know the time of low tide in that part of the world on that night. Then, too, that bell sounded again. And again and again I shouted into the silence. It struck twice this time; but it was not until another half-hour had gone by, and it struck three times with an interval between the second and third strokes, that I realized that somewhere at hand was a ship's bell clock. I yelled for help, calling 'Ship ahoy! Give me a hand here! I'm standing on bottom—on a reef! Lower a boat!'

"Nothing answered me, and I suppose I went more or less crazy as the night went on and that infernal ghostly bell struck off the half-hours. It seemed to have the correct time; but it was hard to realize that a ship had gone through a successful mutiny and shipwreck in the half-hour between eight bells and one bell.

"But it ended at last, when, from the cold and the wet and the strain on my voice, I found myself unable to call out any more. And it struck me as rather hard, too; for at daylight the fog lifted a bit, and there, about a mile and a half to the nor'ard, showed the lug sail of one of the boats. The current must have drifted it to the north during the night, and when the fog lifted I suppose they set the lug and sailed 'fore the wind as the easiest and fastest way to sail.

"But another sight met my eyes! Over to the east about fifty yards was the stern of the ship, taffrail and cabin out, and the mizzentop and topmast. She was just hung there, canted to an angle of forty-five, and ready to slide down with the first shift of a sea. And there was where that clock was, high and dry in the cabin! The tide had reached my shoulders by now, and perhaps this was what did the job; for I suppose there was some air in that wreck, and when an extra heavy pulse of the ground swell came along, there was a slight wrenching sound, as though the sternpost had carried away; then, with a very little flurry, the stern and mizzen sank out of sight.

"But up into the froth and the bubbles caused by the plunge came the red head, anxious face, and big shoulders of Macklin. He sighted me, and came on, breasting the water with all the vigor of a strong man in good form, and with a new look in his face that meant trouble for me. I looked for the boat; but the fog had thickened again, blotting her out.

"'What you got there?' he demanded, as he puffed up close to me.

"'Rock bottom,' I answered. 'Keep off! There's room for only one.'

"'And that one is me!'

"I squared myself as I could, with my bad right hand tucked into my shirt out of the way, and my legs as far apart as I could get them. I struck at him, and pushed him under; but the reacting force of the blow sent me backward, and then it was a mad scramble under water to get my foothold again. Macklin came up, saw me, and swam under water until he had reached my legs; then he hove me off and took my place.

"But he wasn't used to the push of the current, and the next moment he was off and swimming again, while I was on, breasting the current, and waiting for him. He came back under water again; but this time I met him with a kick that sent him so far down as to give me hope he would stay there; but he didn't. He came up, swam around to the south, came down with the current, and brushed me off. I did the same; but he met me with his feet, and I drifted by. However, I had him by the leg with my one good hand, and he came with me. We swam, side by side; but he beat me, and scrambled to his feet on the small spur of rock that meant life to each of us, but not to both. I swam weakly around to the south, and then down on him; realizing that my strength was giving out. But the fight went on, and I soon realized that his gun was soaked, or left behind; otherwise he would have used it before this.

"I have often wondered if God and the angels watched that fight in mid-ocean, or only hell and the devils. The nearest land to the west must have been Cape Race, the nearest to the east the Azores, each about five hundred miles away. I did not know the longitude; but I did know that we had sailed due east since I was disrated, and that then we were on the forty-seventh parallel.

"And so, in latitude forty-seven north, longitude unknown, two weakened human brutes unable to strike a heavy and telling blow, yet animated by a fear of death and love of life that twisted their features into frenzied contortions (I judged mine by Macklin's), struggled feebly for the possession of a mountaintop rising from the sea bed, on the diminishing chance that some ship would come along to the rescue before hunger, thirst, or a rising sea overcame them.

"I hardly know how it ended; I only knew that I found myself too weak to breast the current, and then I gave up, and drifted. I went under twice, I remember, and waited calmly for the end; but before the last sinking I heard voices; then I was clutched by the hair, and as I was dragged bodily into a boat I lost my senses. When I came to, the men lifted me up, and I saw big Finnegan at the tiller, standing erect and declaiming to something astern:

"'Stay there an' think it over, ye man-killin' shlave driver! Stay there, ye devil out o' hell, an' may the min ye've killed come back to kape ye company till yer master comes fur ye!'

"I took one look at Macklin. He was standing erect, breasting the current with his arms folded, secure in the possession of the foothold he had won from me. But he sent no call for help, and soon went out of sight in the thinning fog as the boat sailed away.

"There is little more to this yarn. We never saw the other boat again, and did not know the story they told if rescued. But among ourselves we agreed to say nothing about the mutiny or the shooting or the rock—only that we had struck something submerged, that the ship had sunk, and that the captain, first mate, and three sailors had been drowned. We were picked up in a few days, told this lie, and were not questioned closely. Then I realized why the men had stood by me; they wanted a shipped officer to justify the story.

"But I knew the long arm of the law, and I did not know the fate of the other boat, or the tale they might tell. So, I shipped for the East, found and learned this strait, and have been here since, afraid to go home."

THIS IS THE YARN I listened to on anchor watch thirty years ago. It pertains to events forty years farther back in the past. If that white-haired, mild-mannered old pilot is still alive, he is over ninety-five years old, and immune from earthly punishment.

But, before deciding to give this story to the world, I visited the United States Hydrographic Office for some corroborative data, and on a pilot chart of 1896 read that one Captain Lloyd, of the British ship *Crompton*, had lately reported seeing in latitude forty-seven north and longitude thirty-seven degrees twenty minutes west, a rock sixty feet long and eight or ten feet high in the middle. It was at a time of low spring tides, and such a menace to navigation could easily elude observation under ordinary conditions. Captain Lloyd averred that he saw it at twenty minutes to eight on a fine, sunshiny morning, so close and clear to him that he forbore lowering a boat.

Yet, as I learned from further inquiry, he was the subject of much ridicule, and his story was generally disbelieved.

Should it be disbelieved?

The Argonauts

A few months ago I attended a banquet and left it as I always leave such functions, hungry. Entering an all-night lunch room I took a seat, and gave my order to a waiter, who, when he had filled it, sat down at the table with me. It was very late, and his duties were light.

"You're looking well," he remarked, as his glance traveled over my evening clothes. "You're dead swell, but the last time I saw you, you were covered with mud, carrying a stern line ashore in the Welland Canal."

I took stock of him. He was white-haired, but had the keen, intelligent face of a man of forty-five who had not yet given up the fight; a lively, hopeful face, one that comes to those who win oftener than lose. His skin was brown, as though the sun and wind of all the zones had smitten it. His eyes, gray, steadfast and humorous, had in them when half closed the twinkle of self-confidence, but also, in their wide-open stare, the intensity of a man of initiative and sudden action. In his voice were character, individuality, and the habit of command; yet he wore the short jacket of a waiter, and might have accepted a tip. I could not recall having met him.

"You seem to have the advantage of me," I said. "I know the Welland Canal, however, though I am trying to forget that ditch."

"You can't," he laughed. "No man can who ever went through it. That trip with you in the old *Samana* was my first and last. I struck for salt water again when the old man paid me off at Port Colborne. Don't you remember going to school with me?" He mentioned his name, and with a little effort I recalled him—a schoolmate a little older than myself, who had gone to sea early in life, and returned a full-fledged salt-water navigator, to ship, on his record, as first mate in the schooner that carried me before the mast, and to meet his Waterloo in the Welland Canal, the navigation of which demands qualities never taught nor acquired in the curriculum of sea-faring. After grounding the schooner several times, parting every line on board, and driving us to open revolt by the extra work coming of his mistakes, he was discharged by the skipper. As I thought of all this the grumbling sailor rose within me, and there at the table, he a waiter, I a writer, we fought out a grudge of twenty years' standing. But it ended amicably; I called him a farmer, he called me a soldier, and we shook hands.

"I've learned," he said, as we settled back, "only in the last month or so, that you're the fellow that writes these rotten sea stories. Why don't you write real sea stories?"

"For the same reason that you don't serve a real Welsh rabbit," I answered, tapping the now cold concoction he had served me. "I couldn't sell a real story. Truth is too strange to pose as fiction."

"That's so," he answered, slowly. "Who'd think that you could have become a writer, and I a hash slinger? Making lots of money, I suppose."

"No, I'm not, or I wouldn't be in your society to-night."

"We're all bluffers, I guess. You are, here in this beanery with your glad rags on. I am, too—no, not now. I'm slinging hash, and glad of the chance. But I was a millionaire for a time. Not long. But while it lasted I had dreams—big dreams."

I asked him about this, and there followed his story. It was interrupted every few moments by calls for "ham and—," "corn beef and—," "mystery and white wings," and it kept me at the table until daylight. He preluded it by the advice to write it up as a real sea story, but asked that I suppress his name until he had saved enough to get him to Cuba, where he had new plans for advancement. And now, after months of thought, I am following his advice; for no effort of the creative mind, and no flight of conventional fancy, can equal the weird, grim yarn that he reeled off between orders.

"You must have read in the papers a few weeks back," he began, "about that bunch of college men that chartered the old racer *Mayflower*, filled her up with diving gear and dynamite, and went down after the treasure in the *Santa Margherita*."

I nodded assent. "Yes, and a hurricane hit them and they barely escaped."

"They're keeping mum," he said, "and mean to try again; but it's no use. That treasure is seven hundred miles to the nor-nor'east now, and I was about the last man to look at it. It's resting in the hold of a small schooner, sunk in four hundred fathoms. I never heard of that treasure ship until about three years ago, when I quit a brigantine at Cedar Keys and mixed in with the boarding-house crowd. There was a fellow out of a job named Gleason, and he had a chart in his pocket that he talked about, but never showed. He told us all about that old Spanish ship that went down with all hands in the sixteenth century, carrying with her about seven millions' worth of gold, silver, and jewels; and he knew the location. He had got it from a drunken diver who had seen her on the sea bottom, spelled her dingy old name on the stern, and saved the news to himself while he wormed out of the skipper the latitude and longitude of the place. And now he wanted to enlist capital, or make up a crew of men that would do the work. Dead easy, he said. Just to get there, drag the bottom with two boats and a length of chain until the wreck was located, then to go down in a diving suit, hook on to the chests and hoist them up.

"Well, in the crowd that he talked to there wasn't a dollar. We were all dead broke, but we were all ambitious. There was Pango Pete, a nigger six foot tall, who couldn't write his name, but he was a seaman from his feet up; and a Dago named Pedro Pasqualai. These two were the kind that will choke you before they ask the time of night. Then there was Sullivan, old man Sullivan, a decrepit old codger who had sailed second mate all his life, and never got a first mate's berth because he couldn't master navigation. And there was Peters, a young fellow filled up with the romance and the glory of the life at sea—rot, as you and I know, but he was enthusiastic, and that was enough. A trio of Dutchmen were taken in—Wagner, Weiss, and Myers, three good fellows down on their luck. A Portuguese named Christo, and two Sou'wegian brothers named Swanson completed the bunch. We talked it over down at the end of the fruit dock, where the oyster boats come in and make fast, and where the downs-and-outs congregate to smoke and boast of the prosperous past.

"But this crowd talked of the prosperous future. Seven millions, said Gleason, lay down there off Turks Island in less than sixty fathoms, and all we needed was some kind of a craft to get us there, a diving suit, and a storage battery to light up a bulb to search for the treasure. These things seemed beyond our reach, until a schooner came in for supplies. We sized her up, and Gleason went wild as her different fittings and appliances showed up. There were the diving dresses we needed; there was the storage battery; there were the extra anchors for mooring a craft over a certain spot, and the air pumps and paraphernalia for diving operations, scattered about the deck. She was a small craft, and was manned by men who did not act and talk like sailors. There seemed to be no skipper, and they smoked on deck while working, and talked back and forth as though all were equal.

"'A company,' said Gleason, 'just like us, only they've got the money, and possibly the secret. Well, the company that gets the loot owns it and such matters as the ownership of the schooner and the outfit can be settled afterwards, possibly out of court. What do you say? Are you game?'

"We were. We laid low, but watched, and when that schooner was filled up with grub, we were ready to raid her and chuck the crew overboard; but it wasn't necessary to do the latter. They filled up too late for the tide and went ashore for the evening, leaving no one aboard but a Japanese cook. We remembered, as we climbed aboard after dark, that we hadn't a man among us who could cook, and so, instead of dropping that Jap over the rail, we simply locked him into a stateroom and made sail.

"Naturally, as Gleason originated the scheme, he was elected captain, but, as I was the only navigator in the crowd, I was made first mate, and the big nigger, Pango Pete, second mate. It looked good for discipline, for even pirates recognize the need of it, and the first man that growled or kicked had to deal with Pete. He whaled a few before we'd got around the Florida Cape, but he also whaled the Jap for bad cooking and insolence—which was a mistake. That Jap was an educated man, a college graduate and a member of the Japanese Samurai, a curious class in that country that never yield, never forgive, and kill themselves when defeated. We didn't know this; we only knew that he was a mighty poor cook.

"After we were around the Cape, Gleason gave me the latitude and longitude of the spot, and I made for it. It took me two or three days of careful observations and calculations before I announced that we were within six seconds of the spot, which is all that navigation will do. Then we dropped anchor and began to drag. We knotted together every line we had, and in the middle we had a length of mooring chain that would stick to the bottom. We kept two small boats, to which this was attached, a quarter of a mile apart and pulled on parallel lines, and at last felt a drag; then we pulled together, gathering in the slack, and when we met, the schooner, under charge of Gleason, came up and anchored, over the spot.

"I was the only man there who had any diving experience, so I went down. Say, have you ever been under water in a diving suit, trusting your life to the fellows above who pump the air into your helmet? No? Well, it's a curious experience. I had the feeling as I went down that I was number thirteen of that bunch, and that they only needed to shut off my air supply to make their number twelve instead of thirteen. But that didn't happen; they pumped, and I breathed and saw the old galleon, the *Santa Margherita*. She lay there, heeled over to starboard, covered with the ooze and the slime of the sea, with barnacles everywhere.

"I signaled for slack and walked around her, taking note of her rig. She had three masts, and three tops very much like the fighting tops of our modern battleships. There were no royal masts, but she had two sprit-sail yards under the bowsprit and jib boom, and a huge lateen yard on the mizzen that took the place of the cro'-jack. But her poop deck was a wonder; five tiers of windows one above the other, and on top three big lanterns much like the ordinary street lamp. Of course, all canvas and running gear had rotted away, but here and there was a leg of standing rigging, preserved by the tar. She was a big craft in her day, no doubt, but not so big compared with present-day ships; at any rate I could reach up to her channels, and by this means climbed aboard.

"The deck and rail were a foot thick with mud, and the small, spar-deck guns could hardly be distinguished. I saw at once that I would need help, and signaled to be hauled up. On deck I told the news and all hands, even the Jap, went crazy over it. We got out two more diving suits, rigged a bulb for each, and Pango, Peters, and myself went down again.

"Now, this isn't a yarn of the finding of that treasure. Anyone can invent such yarns, and I've read dozens of them. They all wind up successfully, with each man wealthy and happy. This is a yarn of the men who found that treasure, and what happened to them. So, I'll just say that we didn't find a skeleton or a ghost when we got below decks. All hands were up, I suppose, when that ship went down, and the rush of water as she plunged, washed them off. We found seven big chests in the 'tween-decks forward of the cabin, and in them all were coins, and jewelry, and here and there in the mess, what might have been an opal, or some kind of jewel. All the stuff was black from the action of the salt water; but we knew we had the real thing, and hooked on tackles. We had to come up to help each time we lifted a chest, for, after the chest was out of water, it was too heavy for the crowd above; but at last they were all up, and stowed snugly on the floor of the cabin. Then, after final search for other loot worth taking, we picked up our anchor and cleared out, not yet having decided where we were going.

"We were pirates under the law, and didn't know but what all the revenue cutters on the coast were looking for us, for the theft of that schooner. But with seven millions of bullion and jewels, melted down, counted up, and translated into cash in some bank, we didn't care for the charge of piracy. The real trouble was to get that stuff translated, and while we argued we sailed due east, out into the broad Atlantic. Peters, the young enthusiast, had been a jeweler, and he told us that nothing short of a blast of air in conjunction with the heat of a fire would melt gold and silver. Well, where could we set up a blast furnace with not a dollar in the party? My suggestion—and I was backed by Gleason, Peters, and old man Sullivan—was that we count out the loot, separate every salable jewel, and make some big port like New York, Liverpool, or Rio Janeiro, sell the jewels and get ready money with which to plan for the disposal of the rest; but we had to deal with men like Pango, Christo, Pedro, and the three Dutchmen, who didn't know what they were up against. They wanted an immediate count up and division; then, each man to go his way. The nonsense of it did not strike them; thirteen men to divide up seven heavy chests—each one shouldering seven-thirteenths of a load that took the whole thirteen to lift with a four-fold tackle. We asked the Jap cook what he thought, but he had no opinion.

"It's somewhat curious how the different men of that bunch had different ideas of what they wanted. Young Peters wanted to go back to his native town and win the girl that had soured on him because he was poor. Pango, Pedro, and the two Sou'wegians only wanted a big drunk. Old man Sullivan wanted a course in a Nautical School and a first mate's certificate. The three Germans wanted to get to New York and set up in the saloon business. Gleason wanted to study law, and I wanted to study medicine and be a doctor, a gentleman who could enter any society in the world. The Jap didn't give out his aspirations.

"And so, growling like an unhappy family in a menagerie, we sailed east, with the question unsettled. But at last we won over the Dagoes and the Dutchmen, and agreed upon New York as a port, and the selling of the jewels in some Bowery pawnshop, where no questions are asked. Then we shook hands all round, gave the Jap hell about his cooking—for we had been too worried to attend to that matter before—and squared away before the trade wind for Sandy Hook and a market.

"From jealousy and mutual distrust, we all slept in the cabin. There were plenty of staterooms for the crowd, though some of us doubled up. None of us wanted to remain away from the seven chests of treasure, and the Japanese cook, who might have slept in the cook's room next the galley, still showed a preference for his room in the cabin, and we did not contest it. But now we were millionaires and easy—dead easy. We stood watch, steered and trimmed sail with no man for boss, for now the work was done, Gleason and myself and the nigger Pango gave up our false positions. We were a democracy, and loved and trusted one another, only, when we roused out the watch below and found that old man Sullivan did not come, and on investigation found him stone dead in his berth without a sign of violence, we forgot our brotherly love and began to wonder.

"We did not know what he died of, but we gave him sea burial that day, and Gleason read a chapter from the book. We concluded that the old man had died of heart failure, or old age, and thought no more about it after the day had passed. But, when we called the watch at eight bells next mornin', we couldn't get one of the Swanson brothers up. He was cold and stiff; and there was nothing wrong with him either. That is, he had turned in cheerful and healthy and died during sleep, leaving no sign.

"The other Swanson raised merry hell that day, raving about the deck, mourning for his dead brother. But his grief was short-lived, for when we tried to waken him next watch he was cold and stiff. We buried him with the ceremonies, and began to think—all of us. We wondered whether men may rake up ill-gotten treasure from a dead past without coming under influences of that dead past. We thought of the conquered and enslaved natives, laboring in the mines for the aggrandizement and enrichment of Spain, and giving up their lives in the work, unrecognized and forgotten, while their exploiters, the children and relatives of Ferdinand and Isabella, sat back in luxury and self-satisfaction. We wondered as to what was killing our shipmates, ghosts or poison.

"Naturally, we suspected the cook, and Pango, the Dagoes, and the surviving Sou'wegian were for tossing him overboard; but the rest of us wouldn't have it. There was no evidence of poison, and as we'd done no killing so far in our piratical venture, we'd better keep clear of it now, with so much at stake. A court that would acquit us as soldiers of fortune that had merely borrowed a schooner might hang us as pirates and murderers; but we watched the Jap. We kept him away from the grub while we ate it. He brought it on in two or more big dishes, and there was no chance of his poisoning one without the rest. We weren't afraid of that.

"I examined Swanson thoroughly before we buried him, and there wasn't a mark on him, or a sign of anything out of the way, except what didn't seem in any way important, just below each ear, and back of the corner of the cheek bone, was a little pink spot; but there was no blood, and no sign of finger prints on the throat.

"Peters, the romantic young fellow, got ghosts on his mind, and as he thought about it, they got on his nerves. He couldn't sleep, and walked around, up and down from the cabin to the deck. The others slept in their watch below, and on that night nobody died. But the next night Peters was too exhausted to stay awake, and he went to sleep on the cabin floor alongside the chests. We couldn't waken him at eight bells, and we knew his troubles were over. At daylight I examined his body. Nothing wrong, only the two little pink spots under the ears. We buried him at daylight, with scant pretense of a burial service. Things were looking serious.

"All this time we were plowing along before the trade wind, but it soon panned out and we had light, shifty airs from all directions, with rain—regular Gulf Stream weather. It made us bad-tempered, and Pango and Gleason had a fight. It was a bad fight, and we couldn't stop them; both were powerful men, and as they brushed into me in their whirling lunge along the deck, locked tight, they knocked me six feet away. When I got to my feet, Pango had Gleason down and was choking him. I got a handspike and battered that coon's head with it; but he wouldn't let go, and before others came up to help he had killed him. He went for me, but had to stop before the handspikes of the crowd.

"Now, with Gleason dead, the command devolved upon me or Pango, and this fellow was in a mood to demand the place. He could lick any three of us, but not all hands; but, while we were growling about it and cooling down, we found other troubles to keep us busy. We had piled several tons' weight on the weak cabin floor timbers of an old schooner, and of a sudden, down they crashed to the hold below, leaving a yawning hole in the cabin floor and starting a butt or two in the planking. It was pump, pump, pump, now, for we couldn't rig any kind of a purchase to clear those busted chests away from the leak. Pango was a good worker, and, under the pressure of extreme fatigue, we forgot our grudges. I did not care for the cheap position of command over a bunch of foreigners, and so we made Pango skipper, while I remained navigator and mate. Pango promptly quit pumping, saying that skippers don't pump. And that night he quit everything. As skipper he stood no watch, but at breakfast time he was cold, with the same little marks under his ears. On his skin, however, they showed a brownish black.

"Gleason had been choked to death, and I had examined the imprint of Pango's fingers before we buried him. There was hardly a sign; nothing at all to show that the little pink spots came from the pressure of a strangler's grip. Besides, you cannot choke a man asleep without waking him. He would make some kind of a fuss, and apprise others; but that never happened.

"There were but seven of us now, three Germans, two Dagoes, the Jap, and myself. I talked with that Jap. He was an educated man, highly trained in one of our universities; but he couldn't tell me anything, he said. It was all mysterious and horrible—this quiet taking off of men while they slept. As for poisoning, of which he knew he was suspected, it was absurd. There was no poison on board, to begin with; and why should he, a landsman, seek to poison the men who could take the ship and treasure to port? What could he do alone on the sea? This was logical, and as he was a small, weak, and confiding sort of creature, I exonerated him in my mind from any suspicion of choking the victims.

"That night the two Dagoes, Pedro and Christo, passed into the land beyond. There were the same little marks, but nothing else. Weiss, Wagner, and Myers, the three Germans, got nutty about this time, and talked together in their lingo while they pumped; and when they were alone they talked to themselves. I confess that *I* got nutty. Who wouldn't, with this menace hanging over him? I walked around the deck when I was off pump duty, and I remember that I planned a great school where ambitious young sailor men could study medicine, and escape the drudgery of a life 'fore the mast. Then I planned free eating-houses for tramps, and I was going to use some of my wealth to investigate the private life of a Sunday school superintendent, who, when I was a kid, predicted that I would come to a bad end. You see, we never can judge of our own mental condition at the time. It's only when you look back that you can take stock of yourself. The result of this mental disturbance upon me was insomnia. I couldn't get to sleep; but I kept track of the ship, and worried the three Dutchmen and the Jap into trimming sail when necessary.

"We'd got up to the latitude of the Bermudas, I think, and I was beginning to hope that the curse had left us; for we had passed through three nights without a man dying. But on a stormy morning, when the gaff topsails were blown away, and we four men—for the Jap was useless on deck—were trying to get a couple of reefs in the mainsail, Wagner suddenly howled out a lot of Dutch language and jumped overboard. I flung him a line, but he wouldn't take it, and passed astern. The poor devil had taken the national remedy for trouble. Did you ever notice it in Germans, even the best? When things go wrong they kill themselves. They're something like the Chinese in this.

"There were only four of us now, counting the Jap, who still spoiled good grub, and it took a long time to snug that schooner down to double reefs and one head sail. The water in the hold had gained on us, and we pumped while we could stand it, then knocked off, and dropped down on deck for a snooze. We were dead beat, and told the cook to call us if the wind freshened or if anything happened. He didn't call us, but something happened. I wakened in time, and stood up, sleepy and stupid and cold; for you can't sleep on deck, even in the tropics, without getting chilled; and we were up to thirty-six north. The Jap was fooling round the galley, and the schooner, with the wheel becketed, was lifting up and falling off, practically steering herself, by-the-wind. Of course, I thought of the water in the hold, and sounded the well. There was four feet of wet line, and I knew that things were bad. Then I went to the two Dutchmen, to call them to the pumps, and found them cold and stiff, each with the little pink marks under the ears.

"Well, I naturally went more or less crazy. I took that Jap by the throat and asked him what had happened. He did not know, he said. He had left us to sleep, and rest, sorry for us, and trying to cook us a good meal when we wakened. He was in a shaking fright, trembling and quavering, and I eased up. What was the use of anger and suspicion in the face of this horrible threat of death while you slept? We hove the two bodies overboard, and made a stagger at the pump; but we could not lessen the water in the hold, and at last I gave up, cleared away a boat, and stocked it with water and grub for two. Meanwhile I shaped a course for the Bermudas, and steered it after a fashion, hoping that I might beach the schooner and get, out of some court of salvage, a part of that seven millions down in the hold.

"But I had to steer, and keep the deck, for the Jap was useless. I kept it up until we sighted land, and then flopped, done up, tired out, utterly exhausted by work, and yet unable to sleep. I sang out to the cook, as I lay down on the hatch, to try and steer toward that blot of blue on the horizon, and then passed into a semi-dazed state of mind that was not sleep, nor yet wakefulness. I could hear, and, through my half-opened eyelids, could see; yet I was not awake, for I could not guard myself. I saw that Jap creeping toward me. I saw the furtive, murderous glint in his beady eyes. I heard the soft pat of his feet on the wet deck, and I heard his suppressed breathing. But I could not move or speak.

"He came and stood over me, then reached down and softly pressed the tips of his forefingers into my throat, just below the ears and back of the cheek bones. Softly at first, so that I hardly felt it, then more strongly, and a sense of weakness of body came over me, something distinct from the weakness that I had felt while sinking down to try and sleep. It seemed a stopping of breath. I could not move, as yet, but could see, out of the corners of my eye, and a more hateful, murderous face never afflicted me than the face of that Japanese cook.

"He kept it up, steadily increasing the pressure, and soon I realized that I was not breathing. Then, I do not know why, there came to me the thought of that Sunday school superintendent, and his advice, to pray when in trouble. I forgot my grouch. I said to myself, 'God help me, God help me,' and I wakened. I found that I could move. I shook off the Jap, and he staggered back, chuckling and cluttering in his language. I rose to my feet, weak and shaky, and he ran away from me; but I found myself without power to follow. I was more than weak; I was just alive, just able to breathe, but I could not speak. I tried to, but the words would not come. He shut himself into his galley, and, with regard to the condition of the schooner, and my own helplessness, I painfully climbed into the boat I had stocked and cleared away the davit falls. Then I lay down.

"I have a dim remembrance of that sleep in the boat, of waking occasionally to drive that cowardly Jap off with an upraised oar; of my utter inability to speak to him, and the awful difficulty of taking a long breath. But the final plunge of the schooner stands out. I was awake, or as nearly awake as I could be. The Jap was forward, and the decks were awash. I knew that she was going down, and got out my knife to cut the falls when the boat floated. I did this successfully, for, though I could not speak, I could move, and as the schooner plunged under, and the screams of that heathen rang in my ears, I cut the bow tackle, then the stern tackle, and found myself adrift in a turmoil of whirlpools.

"I was picked up a few days later by a fruiter, and taken into New York. I found my hair had turned white. I've been working as waiter most of the time since, hoping to enlist somebody's interest toward salving that schooner; but it's no go. I'm going to Cuba, where I've heard of a pot of money in the Santiago hills. Want to go along?"

"No," I answered. "But, tell me, what killed those men?"

"The Jap must have been an expert in jiu jitsu, the wrestling game of that country. I've made a stagger at studying medicine since then, and learned a little. The pneumogastric nerve did the business. It passes from the base of the brain, down past the heart and lungs and ends near the stomach. It is motor, sensory, and sympathetic, all in one. Gentle pressure inhibits breathing, continued pressure, or stimulus, paralyzes the vocal chords; a continuance of the stimulus renders you unconscious, and a strong pressure brings about stoppage of the heart action, and death."

The Married Man

He told the story while he and I smoked at one end of his veranda, and his kindly faced wife talked with "the only girl on earth" at the other end, beyond reach of his voice. He was a large, portly, and benign old gentleman, with an infinite experience of life, whom I had long known as a fellow-tenant in the studio building. He was not an artist, but an editorial-writer on one of the great dailies, who worked, cooked, and slept in his studio, until Saturday evening came, when he regularly disappeared, until Monday morning.

There was nothing in this to surprise me, until he invited the only girl and myself to visit his country home over Sunday, incidentally informing us that he was a married man, and had been for more than twenty years.

And we found him most happily married. Indeed, he and his white-haired wife were so foolishly fond of each other that their caresses would have seemed absurd had they not been so genuine.

These old lovers had made much of us; and they seemed so sincerely interested in our coming marriage that, in the evening, as night settled over the quiet little suburb, and we sought the veranda for coolness, I ventured to comment to my host on his mode of life.

"Best plan in the world," he answered. "You'll find it so, after a year or two of creative work at home. Don't give up your studio. If you do, you will suffer—as I did before I began my double life—from nervous prostration. I was writing when I married—long-winded essays, sermons, editorials, and arguments about nothing at all, simply built up from the films of my imagination. The thousand-and-one distractions of household life interfered too much, and the more I tried to force my brain the more I fatigued it. The result was that I had a bad six months with myself, and then gave out, just on the verge of insanity.

"Yes, my home life nearly maddened me, as I have said. Then, I took a studio, lived in it, and visited my wife twice a week. The result was that I got my work done, and found my wife as glad to see me as I was to see her. It was like a lad's going to see his girl; and, talk as you like about conjugal bliss, a woman gets tired of a man about the house all day long. Still, there is a danger attached to this dual residence. One must walk straight, for he is a marked man. I had an experience at the beginning that taught me the need of prudence.

"It was while I was mentally convalescent, but yet a very weak man, nervous, irritable, and of unsound judgment. There was about the same kind of a crowd in the building as now—artists, musicians, actors, and actresses. There were women coming and going at all hours, and all sorts of shady characters had access to the place. One day a neighbor named Bunker brought a pleasing young person in black into my place, and introduced us. She was the widow, she informed me, of a newspaper man, who often, when alive, had spoken of me. So hearing that I was in the building, she had asked her friend, Mr. Bunker, to bring us together, as she wished to know her dear husband's friends. She wiped away a tear at this point—genuine, too.

"Now, I had no remembrance of her husband, but, feeling kindly toward any newspaper man's widow, I welcomed her, and Bunker left us together. She was intelligent, with literary aspirations, and we chatted a while very agreeably. Then she borrowed a book, and left.

"I had noticed that, though neatly dressed, her clothing was palpably cheap in quality, and, when she came again—without Bunker, this time—it seemed a little more worn than was consistent with good times. So I questioned her gently, and learned that she had eaten nothing that day. She was trying to make her way by writing short stories, and that fact aroused my pity—a pity that grew when I saw her eat the luncheon I provided from my ice-box.

"She did not come again for a month, and then she appeared with the blackest eye I had ever seen on a woman. She was seedier than ever, and looked hungry. I was deeply sorry for her, believing her clothing a sure index of an honest woman's struggle to remain honest. Partly from the delicacy of feeling due to this belief, and partly because I had but thirty-five cents in my pocket, I made no offer of pecuniary assistance. But, after giving me a conventional explanation of the cause of the black eye, she hinted plainly that, unless she could raise ten dollars before night, she would be turned out of her room. This was serious, and I took thought.

"It was Friday, and a holiday. I knew that there was no one in the building but Bunker and myself, and Bunker was one of those rollicking souls who are in a continuous condition of cheerful impecuniosity. There was not a place open in the neighborhood except the saloons, and there I was not known. Clearly, I could not raise any money for her that day; but I promised her the use of my studio for the two following nights, when I should be home in the country, and I agreed to induce

Bunker, who slept in his boarding-house, to put her up in his place for that night. This would provide sleeping quarters and the use of my gas-stove and ice-box for three nights and two days, by which time something might turn up. She expressed herself as satisfied, and I went out to interview Bunker.

"'No,' he declared, vehemently, 'I can't take any woman to my place.' 'Bunker,' I interrupted, solemnly, 'you brought this young woman here, you have pretended to be her friend, and her claim upon you is enough to warrant her in expecting help at this critical moment. Remember, Bunker, this is a crisis with her. If she is helped, she may pull through; if not, she may lose heart and courage, and go to ruin.'

"My words impressed him. 'All right,' he said; 'I don't know much about her lately—knew her family well, out West—that's all. I'll give you my key, before I go home—want to lock myself in and work for a while now. Have a drink. Got some good stuff here.'

"I declined, and went back to my visitor, picking up on the way a telegraph messenger, who had arrived with a dispatch for me.

"Unwearied in well-doing, glad that I was an instrument in helping this worthy young woman, I assured her of the success of my mission—before opening the telegram. And she thanked me, with tears—genuine again. Then, slightly affected myself, I broke the envelope, and read:

Meet me 5.30 Pennsylvania ferry. If miss you will come to your office.

Maud Milner

"Now, Maud Milner was the wife of an old friend of mine; and, too, she was my wife's old school chum. She had never been in New York, and she did not know that my 'office' was a bachelor's apartment. But her visit had been prearranged, and I had written the invitation on my studio stationery, so that her response was quite innocent; yet, I had peculiar reasons—aside from the presence there of my penniless and interesting protégée—for not wishing her to visit my place in town.

"I had paid her fully as much attention before her marriage as I had my wife; in fact, I courted them both at once, in order to arouse their sense of pique. Not a strictly honorable thing to do, had either of them cared for me, initially; but neither did care, and I might not have won my wife by any other plan. The two were bad friends for a while, and, to this day, my wife cannot rid herself of a very slight jealousy. So, you see the reason for my anxiety to avoid any possibility of complications.

"I had just enough time in which to get to the ferry, and, after emphasizing to the widow the necessity of her getting Bunker's key before he left, and of leaving my studio empty against the possible arrival of Mrs. Milner without me, I rushed away.

"I reached the ferry on time; but Mrs. Milner was not there, nor did she come, though I waited until seven o'clock. Then I inquired, and an official informed that the five-thirty—the train boat—had met with an accident, and had landed her passengers at the nearest dock, which was a little further up. I hurried there, but Mrs. Milner was not visible. At last, fearing lest she had gone to the studio, and had met the widow with that picturesque black eye, I hastened uptown again.

"At the street-door I met Bunker—drunk as a lord.

"'Is she up there yet?' I asked, anxiously.

"'Who?' he answered, in a tone that told me he had forgotten.

"'Did you give her your key? Give me that key—the key of your studio. Hurry up!'

"A dim light of intelligence flashed over his cheerful face, and he grinned.

"'Oh, yesh—yesh; thash so!' He pulled out a bunch of keys. 'Here's keys, ol' man—street-door key and studio key.'

"As he staggered off, I bounded up the stairs, with the two keys he had pulled from his bunch.

"The widow met me at my door.

"'Has a lady called here?' I asked, hastily.

"'Somebody peeped in,' she said. 'It may have been a lady, but I thought it was Mr. Bunker, and as soon as I could—I was dressing my eye—I followed out; but he was gone.'

"'Oh, Lord!' I groaned. 'If it was she, she's gone out to my place, and she will tell my wife.'

"Then I remembered that Mrs. Milner did not have my country address, and was comforted.

"But I had been extremely agitated, and now my shattered nervous system went back on me so completely that I practically turned that interesting female out.

"'The lady may come back at any moment,' I said. 'Here are the keys—this one for the outer door, this one for the studio. Don't let her find you with me in this place.'

"I gave the widow the keys, and she left, saying that she would make a call on someone who had promised her employment, and that she would not annoy me further. She was extremely grateful for my kindness, and all that.

"I hurried her out; and, after a while, settled down to my desk, and worked through the evening—worked hard, to keep from worrying over the whereabouts of Mrs. Milner, alone in that great city.

"Mrs. Milner quite failed to appear; but, at eleven o'clock the other one came. I heard her in the hall, fumbling at the keyhole of Bunker's door, and went out.

"'This key will not unlock the door,' she said, and I joined her.

"Trying the key, I found that it did not fit—in fact, that it was a key shaped differently from all other door-keys in that building; and I knew that the befuddled Bunker had made a mistake.

"'He gave you the right key for the street-door,' the widow whimpered; 'why did he give the wrong one for this door?'

"'Drunk,' I growled. 'Come in, and we'll talk it over.'

"'Oh, I cannot,' she complained. 'To think of it! the terrible position I am in! Oh, to think of it!'

"'Don't think of it,' I answered; 'it's all right. Don't think of it, and don't talk of it. I'll say nothing, and I'll go home as soon as I've finished the page I'm on. Come in and sit down.'

"I led her in, and sat her down, but her plaint would not cease. I fancied there was a smell of liquor in the air, but I could not be sure that it was not the clinging odor left by Bunker. I turned to my work, and endeavored to write, but could not; for now her mood changed to one of patronage, and she advised me upon my methods, my style of writing, my manner of living. She promised to be a friend to me all her life. She would help me to reform my rather slap-dash style of writing, and to give it the literary touch, and she would help me in my punctuation. She had made a study of my editorials, and knew all my weak points.

"All this was enough to exasperate a steadier-nerved man than myself. It drove me, barely convalescent from mental collapse, to distraction.

"'Here,' I said, rudely, standing up, 'you will not stop talking, so I must stop work. I'll give it up and go home.'

"'Oh, don't let me disturb you,' she said, pleadingly, as she, too, rose and approached me; 'I will be quiet, I really will.'

"But I smelt the odor of liquor again now plainly from her breath, and I did not believe that she could stop talking if she tried. My resolution to go was made stronger.

"I went to a cabinet at the far end of the studio, to get some papers I wished to carry home with me. I returned quickly.

"But, in that short time, she had made changes; she had laid aside her hat and jacket when she came in, but now she stood before my mirror, shaking her hair down her back, and unbuttoning her collar. She smiled sweetly as she turned to me.

"Without a word, I caught up my hat, and fled.

"Down in the street, I looked at my watch. It was nearly midnight. It would take me until two in the morning to get home, where I would have to wake my wife, and relate the whole truth—or else tell her a lie as to why I was home a day ahead of time. I cared to do neither, and thought of a hotel. But, though I had a commutation ticket in my pocket, my money was now reduced to twenty-five cents—not enough to pay for a night's lodging. There was not a soul left in that darkened building to whom I could appeal.

"Then I bethought me of a friend of many years' standing, who lived on the top floor of a bachelor apartment not far away. With my grip in my hand, I hurried to his street, and was taken up by the elevator to the top floor, dimly lighted and bordered with doors.

"I knew his door, and knocked on it. There was no answer. I knocked again and again, but he did not respond. At last, in desperation, I rang for the elevator, and asked the attendant where my friend was. The boy did not know, but thought that the gentleman must be in, and asleep.

"However, I went down, and waited for a half-hour at the door, hoping that he had been out late and would soon appear. But he did not, and I went up again, resolved to batter down his door, if necessary. I began the attack at once, and, though I produced no effect on the door, I did upon my knuckles and the repose of other tenants of the floor. Doors opened, and tired, sleepy voices inquired the reason of the tumult. I made no answer, but banged away.

"'Tom,' I shouted, at last; 'Tom, get up! Let me in! I want to see you; it's important. Let me in!'

"A voice from a half-opened door informed me that if I did not stop the noise I should be pitched down the stairs. Still, I banged away at Tom's door. There was no response, and I grew sick at heart.

"Then, just as I was about to go away, a door leading up to the attic opened, and Tom appeared, clad in street clothing—overcoat and all.

"'What's up?' he inquired, with chattering teeth.

"'Tom!' I exclaimed, reaching his side at a bound, 'I want to talk with you. Take me into your place. I'm in trouble. I want to sleep in your room with you. Take me in.'

"'Come upstairs,' he said, calmly.

"I followed him up to the bare and chilly attic, where he lighted a candle, and offered me a seat—on the floor. I told him my agonized tale of woe, but he did not show the sympathy I had anticipated; in fact, he laughed, softly and long.

"'You can sleep with me, if you insist,' he said. 'I've a Persian rug that will almost cover us both, and I'll share this pillow with you. Then, here's a single portière—not very warm—and two New York *Heralds* and a Sunday *Times* that will help out. But, in fact, I'd rather not entertain you to-night. I'd rather you'd go out and walk the street, or sleep in the Park. I couldn't sleep a wink myself with you alongside of me, and neither could you.'

"'But your room,' I gasped; 'what's the matter with your room?'

"'I've been turned out of my room,' he said. 'I'm allowed to sleep here, to-night; and I don't know how it will be to-morrow night—can't tell.'

"'Well, I'll bunk in with you, here.'

"'No,' he rejoined, heartlessly; 'on the whole, I don't want you. Get out and walk the street, or try someone else.'

"'Then lend me some money. I'll go to a hotel.'

"'If I had any money, do you think I should be sleeping here, to-night?'

"'I suppose not,' I sighed. 'Well, I think I'll go. You won't help me?'

"'Not this night,' he said, grimly. 'Get out! But I don't want you to gabble about where you found me sleeping.'

"I left him, deeply grieved by his meanness, which I ascribed to an old jealousy of the years gone by, when he had been attentive to the unmarried Mrs. Milner, and had found me in his way. I had not thought he would have cherished this spite through the years, but, resolved never to ask a favor again, I left him, and went out into the street. Finally, unable to think of another resource, I sought the nearest square, and put in a cold and miserable night on a bench, with vagrants, beggars, and outcasts for company.

"At daylight, I rose and wandered slowly back toward the studio building, to await the down-coming of my charge.

"At the door I met a disheveled, weary, and bleary-eyed wreck, who eyed me sourly, and broke forth.

"'You're a nice sort of duffer, you are,' he said. 'You knew I was drunk. You knew I didn't know what key I gave you. Why didn't you make sure? I couldn't get into my boarding-house. I walked the street all night.'

"'You did!' I responded. 'You walked the street all night, did you? Oh, I'm so glad! I'm *so* glad, Bunker! You walked the street, did you? Well, I slept in the square—thanks to your condition, you unholy inebriate!'

"'Where's my key?' he demanded, angrily, 'my boarding-house key? I want to get in before breakfast-time.'

"'Up in my studio,' I answered, fully as tartly. 'Go up there and trade keys; and don't bring any more of your friends around to me.'

"I went to a restaurant, spent my twenty-five cents for breakfast, and then climbed to the studio. The door was unlocked, but the bird had flown.

"I spent a miserable day, doing no work at all, but worrying greatly over the fate of Mrs. Milner.

"But, at nightfall, having replenished my pockets from the bank, as I was about to leave the building, to take the train for home, I met her, bag and baggage in a cab at the door.

"Did you ever get a thorough scolding from an angry woman, or, as in this case, from a good-natured woman pretending to be angry? But, alas! I did not know that she was pretending, and I suffered horribly—on the ride to the station and on the train. I was an unfaithful, treacherous scoundrel, leaving a trusting and loving wife alone for a whole week, and giving the use of 'my office'—in which there was a couch and an ice-box and a gas-stove and a bath-tub and a clothes-closet (*for hiding purposes*)—to a shameless person with a black-and-blue eye, who had stared at her most insolently when she had come to the door.

"'I mean to tell your wife,' Mrs. Milner said, before we had reached the Grand Central Station; and she repeated the threat a dozen times, before we arrived at my house. Then, on the walk home, I, who had maintained a moody silence all the way, plucked up heart, in the effort to compose myself for the meeting with my wife, and asked her how she had managed herself.

"'I,' she answered, with feminine scorn, 'I was turned away from three hotels, before I finally understood your generous metropolitan hotel rules, which doom traveling women to the police-stations for lodging. I should have walked the streets, if I had not met a friend who generously took me home with her.'

"'I hope you slept well,' I ventured, miserably.

"'I did not! Her apartments were 'way up at the top of a big, high building; and, just as I got to sleep, there was a frightful banging at the door, and a man—a drunken man, evidently—shouted to be let in. "Tom," he howled, "Tom, get up! Let me in! I want to see you; it's important. Let me in!" Now, of course, there was no "Tom" there, so I just lay quiet, frightened to death, however; and, at last, the drunken brute went away. But I did not sleep a wink, thanks to you and your indifference toward my safety, and your devotion to creatures who get black eyes. Oh, I'll tell your wife! I'll let her know!'

"We were under a street-lamp, and I pulled her to a stop, turning her around, so that the light shone squarely on her face.

"'Maud,' I said, and I shook my forefinger at her, 'you will not tell my wife. You will be a good and humble young woman during your stay with us; yes, you will. You will be very discreet and very forgiving. If you are not, I shall tell your husband that you spent last night in the apartments of my friend Tom, your old lover.'

"And did you ever see a woman blush, my boy?—not the blush she puts on at will, but a blush that is genuinely in earnest—a blush she cannot help. I had my revenge as I watched her blush. She blushed in seven colors—every color in the spectrum. Then she turned loose on Tom—an honorable fellow, poor devil, sleeping in that cold garret for her sake—and scourged him for telling me.

"But I stopped her with the information that I was the drunken brute who had banged on the door, to which I added the fiction that I had seen her go in.

"Well, we patched up a truce before we reached home, and we are good friends to-day. Tom married her, after her husband died; and, to this day, he is somewhat embarrassed in my presence, feeling, no doubt, that I do not forgive his heartlessness to me on that night. I cannot explain, and, somehow, his wife will not. I don't know why, unless it is because she has a generous streak in her makeup, and thinks that it will involve revelations concerning the person with the black eye."

"And could you not convince Mrs. Milner of the truth of the affair?" I asked.

"Tried to—tried hard—but she did not believe me; or, at least, said she did not."

"And did you ever see the interesting widow again?"

"Many times—but she never saw me!"

We smoked, silently—he, straight-faced and reminiscent, I, smiling over the story he had told.

"May I tell this experience to the girl over yonder?" I asked.

"Well, yes; but, as I never told my wife, put the girl on her honor not to repeat it. It may help you in your adjustment of your married life; it may convince her that a man can be trusted out of his home."

THE TRIPLE ALLIANCE

Two men walked side by side down the steps of the Criminal Court Building. They were dressed in "store clothes"; and, while they were alike in type, yet they were unlike: one could not be mistaken for the other. But they had the same facial angle; they were of about the same age, thirty-five; each was tall, square-shouldered, and erect, and each had the same curious gait that betokens long experience in the saddle. The man to the right had gray eyes; the one to the left black. The one to the right was jubilant of face; the other downcast and chagrined. As they reached the sidewalk a man hurried out of the crowd and confronted them. His face was perspiring, and he breathed hard.

"I've got you, Bill!" he said, laying his hand on the shoulder of the downcast man to the left. "You're my prisoner!"

"Not much, he isn't!" answered the man to the right. "He's mine. Here's proof." He half turned, disclosing the butt of a large pistol under his coat.

"Oh, I've got that kind of proof, too," rejoined the newcomer, stepping back and eying them with anger and disgust in his face. It was a face that must have been unused to such emotional expressions; it was smooth shaved, pink, and healthy, with keen blue eyes, the face of a man not yet grown up, or of a boy matured before his time. He was of about the same age, size, and build as the other two, and with the same horseman's gait.

"Who are you," he asked, "and what have you got that man for?"

"I'm Jack Quincy, Deputy Sheriff of Maricopa County, Arizona; and I've got this man, Bill Rogers, for stage robbery. Who are you?"

"I'm Walter Benson, of the Northwest Mounted Police, and I want this man for murder. I've just come from Washington with extradition papers, and I don't see how you can hold him."

"Possession is nine points of the law in this country, Mr. Benson, and, while I only went to Albany for extradition papers, they're good. Left 'em inside with the Judge."

"I'll contest this case. I've come down from Manitoba for this man. My chief put the New York police onto him, and he's our meat. Why, man, we want him for murder, a capital offense!"

"But I've got him for robbing the Wickenburg stage, a capital offense, too."

While this confab was going on the prisoner had been keenly and furtively looking about, and had caught the eye of a nearby policeman, then had significantly reached his hand behind him and patted his hip pocket while nodding almost imperceptibly toward the disputants. The officer summoned another policeman by the same sign language, and at this juncture they approached.

"What you two chewin' the rag about?" demanded one, passing his hands rapidly up and down and around the rear clothing of Quincy, while the other as quickly "frisked" Benson. "Got a gun, I see! Got a license?"

"Here's another gun man," said the second policeman, his hand on Benson's collar. "Got a license?"

"Yes, where's yer license?" repeated the first officer, reaching for Quincy's collar.

And now a surprising thing happened. First, Bill Rogers, wanted for stage robbery and murder, took to his heels and sped down the street. Then Benson wriggled under the policeman's grasp, and by some lightning-like trick of jiu jitsu, sent him sprawling on his back, his limbs waving in the air like the legs of a turtle similarly upset. Then Benson started after Rogers. Quincy tried no jiu jitsu: instead he whipped out his gun, a long, heavy Colt's forty-five, and jammed it into the policeman's face before the hand had reached his collar. Involuntarily the officer started back, away from that murderous blue tube, and before he could recover from his surprise Quincy had started after Benson. Then the policeman followed Quincy, and his fallen compatriot, picking himself up, followed after; but neither for long; they were fat, and these men of the West could run as well as ride.

Down Centre Street went the chase, pursued and pursuers bowling over pedestrians who got in the way, dodging in front of and around trolley cars as Rogers led the way diagonally across the street. He turned into the first cross street and reached Park Row, Benson about a hundred feet behind, and Quincy as far in the rear of Benson. Across Park Row went Rogers, and down the eastern walk to Catharine Street, into which he turned, Benson after him, and Quincy keeping Benson in sight. Rogers seemed to know where he was going. He raced down Catharine Street into Cherry, and when halfway to the next corner burst into a small saloon, whose proprietor, a large, beetle-browed man, stood behind the bar.

"Sailors' boarding-house, isn't it?" panted Rogers. "Hide me and ship me! I've been to sea. North America's too hot for me."

"Yes," responded the proprietor, with quick comprehension. "Into that back room and up the stairs. Hide anywhere. I'll stall the police."

But before Rogers could reach the back room Benson burst in, his blue eyes flashing with excitement, and in his hand a revolver as large and heavy as Quincy's.

"Hold on, Bill!" he snapped. "Hands up! I've got a bead on you!"

Rogers halted and turned, his hands over his head and his features drooping in despair. Benson, still covering him, advanced and laid hold of his collar. Then in burst Quincy, also with drawn revolver.

"Got him, have you? Good enough! I'll take him."

"Oh, no, you won't," answered Benson. "He's mine. Possession's nine points of the law, you say." With his hand still on Rogers's collar he covered Quincy with his weapon.

Quincy had not raised his; and he stood still, leaning forward, his pistol pointed to the floor, while he glared at Benson.

"Now, then, stop this!" said the proprietor, sternly, as he leveled a bright, nickel-plated revolver at Benson. "Lower that gun—quick! Lower it—"

Benson saw out of the corner of his eye, and slowly lowered the pistol.

"You, too," he said to Quincy, as he looked at him. "Don't you raise that shootin' iron! I'm boss here. Put 'em both on the bar, handles first, both of you!"

There was deadly earnestness in the big man's voice, and they obeyed him. Handles first the weapons were placed on the bar. Then Quincy said:

"You're makin' trouble for yourself. This man is my prisoner, and you're interfering with an officer."

"You a p'liceman?" asked the big man, as he placed the weapons under the bar.

"I'm Deputy Sheriff of Maricopa County, Arizona."

"And I'm a member of the Northwest Mounted Police," said Benson.

"You're a long way from home, and you've got no friends here. This man has. He says he's a sailor, and I'm a friend o' sailors. Been one myself, and I make my livin' off 'em. And when a sailor runs into my place askin' to hide from anyone, police or not, I'm on his side every time."

"He's no sailor," said Quincy. "He's Bill Rogers, an outlaw I came East for."

"How about it?" asked the proprietor, turning to Rogers. "You a sailor?"

"Have been. Can be again," answered Rogers calmly.

"Box the compass."

"North, nor'-an'-by-east, nor'-nor'east, nor'east-an'-by—"

"That's good. Which side does the main topgallant halyards lead down?"

"Port side. Fore and mizzen to starboard."

"This man's a sailor, all right. And he's not goin' out o' my place under any man's gun, 'less he's a policeman with a warrant."

"Well, we'll get the policeman with a warrant," said Quincy, "unless this will do." He drew forth a receipt made out by the clerk of the court for extradition papers.

Benson stiffened up. "Here's something better," he said: "Extradition papers issued by the authorities at Washington. It's a warrant, if anything is." He drew forth his evidence of official integrity.

The big man examined both. "Beyond me, just now," he commented. "However, I'm not goin' to see a sailor railroaded out o' my place till I'm sure it's all right. Come into the back room. We'll all have a drink and talk it over. Casey!" he yelled at the top of his voice, and when a voice from upstairs answered he added: "Come down here an' tend bar."

Casey, a smaller edition of the proprietor, appeared, and the three men were led to the back room, where they seated themselves at a round table, while the proprietor himself took their orders. The drinks were soon served, the big man bringing one for himself, and joining them.

"Now, then," he said, lifting his glass, "we'll drink to a good-natured settlement o' this job. What's this man done out West?"

They all drank.

"Robbed the Wickenburg stage of the first cleanup of Jim Mahar's placer mine. About ten thousand dollars he got away with."

"Jim Mahar!" said Benson. "Why, that's the name of the man he murdered in Manitoba."

"How about it, mate?" said the big man, turning to Rogers.

"Same man," he said quietly. "I shot him; but I never robbed him."

"You didn't?" answered Quincy, derisively. "You were recognized!"

"The mine was mine, and the dust I took I had washed out with my own hands. He got that mine away from me on a technicality, Quincy, and you know it."

MORGAN ROBERTSON

"Oh, I know there was some dispute; but that's not my business. I'm here to take you back, and I've got to do it."

"What's the use," said Benson, "if you haven't got a clear case against him? Now, I have. He shot Mahar on sight, in the presence of a dozen witnesses."

"You mean," said Rogers, "that I was quickest. He pulled first; but I beat him to it, that's all."

"Well," said the big proprietor, "we'll have to think on this a little. So, let's do a little thinking."

They responded to the extent of doing no more talking. Yet it could hardly be said that they were thinking. A fog closed down on their faculties, the room and its fittings grew misty, and in a few moments Benson's head sagged to the table, Quincy lay back in his chair, and Rogers slid to the floor.

"Casey," called the big man, and Casey appeared. "You needn't go to South Brooklyn for the three men we need for the crew to-morrow mornin'. Here's three. One's a sure sailorman, anxious to ship, and the other two'll do. Get Tom to help you upstairs with 'em and get 'em ready. You know the trick. Change their clothes, give 'em a bagful each, and dip their hands in that tar bucket, then wipe most of it off with grease. Get some from the kitchen."

And so were shanghaied a Deputy Sheriff of Arizona, a member of the Northwest Mounted Police, and a desperate outlaw and fugitive from justice.

They wakened about ten next morning with throbbing headaches, and clad in greasy canvas rags, each stretched out in a forecastle bunk with a bag of other greasy rags for a pillow. Rogers was the first to roll out, and after a blear-eyed inspection of the forecastle, which included the other two, he exclaimed, "Well, I'll be blanked!" Then he shook each into sitting posture, listened to their groaning protests, and sat down on a chest, shaking with silent laughter, while the other two resumed the horizontal.

But he did not laugh long. Certain sounds from on deck indicated that he would soon be wanted, and certain indications of wintry weather in the shape of snow flurrying into the forecastle reminded him of his raiment. He hauled out the clothes bag from his bunk and opened it. To his surprise he found, neatly folded, his suit of store clothes; but as this would not do for shipboard wear he sought farther, and found a warm monkey jacket and guernsey, the property, no doubt, of some sailor who had died in the boarding-house or run away from his board bill. He also found a note addressed to Bill Rogers, which he read, and again exclaimed, "I'll be blanked!" adding to it, however, the comment, "A square boarding master." Then he punched and felt of the bag's contents, and smiled.

Donning the guernsey and jacket, he went on deck just in time to meet a big, bearded man who was hurrying to the forecastle door.

"So, you've sobered up, have you?" he said. "Got the whisky out o' you?"

"Wasn't whisky, Sir," answered Rogers, recognizing an officer. "I was doped and shanghaied, even though willing to ship. I'm an able seaman, Sir."

"You don't look it."

"Fifteen years at sea, Sir, though the last ten ashore. I'm a bit tender; but I know my work."

"How about the other two? Are they sailors?"

"I don't think they are, Sir," answered Rogers, with a slight grin. "They were with me when I was doped; but I don't know much about them."

"Go aft and take the wheel. There's a farmer there that can't steer. Let's see what you can do. I'll tend to your friends."

Rogers went to the wheel, received the spokes and the course from the rather distressed incumbent, and, even though the ship was riding along before a stiff quartering breeze and following sea, steered a course good enough to win silence from the skipper—another big, bearded man—when he next looked into the binnacle. Silence, on such occasions, is a compliment.

The cold, fresh breeze soon cleared Rogers's head of its aches and throbs, and he took stock of the ship and her people. She seemed to be about twelve hundred tons' register, with no skysails, stunsails, or other kites to make work for her crew, an easy ship, as far as wind and weather were concerned. Rogers counted her crew—sixteen men scattered about the decks and rigging, lashing casks, stowing lines and fenders, and securing chafing gear aloft. The big man that had spoken to him was undoubtedly the first mate, as was evidenced by his louder voice. The second mate, a short, broad, square-jawed man with a smooth face, spoke little to the men, but struck them often. Rogers saw three floored before six bells. As for the crew, they were of all nations and types, and by these signs he knew that she was an American ship; but nothing yet of her name or destination. Astern was a blue spot on the horizon which he recognized as the Highlands of Navesink, and scattered about at various distances were out- and in-bound craft, sail and steam. But none was within hailing range.

Just before noon he saw two men thrown out of the forecastle by the huge first mate, and in spite of their canvas rags he recognized his two enemies. Involuntarily Rogers smiled; but the smile left his face when he saw that they were showing fight, and that in the fight they were being sadly bested by the mate, aided by his confrère, the second officer. Yet they fought as they could, and as the whirl of battle drifted aft Rogers could hear their voices.

"I want to see the Captain!" they each declared explosively, whenever a moment's respite enabled them to speak, and in time the reiterated demand bore results. The Captain himself appeared, watched the conflict for a moment, then roared out:

"Mr. Billings, that'll do! Send those men up here, and let's see what they want."

The two mates stood back, and the disfigured Sheriff of Maricopa and the almost unrecognizable mounted policeman climbed the poop steps and faced the Captain in the weather alley. They were game—still full of fight, and in no way abashed by the autocrat of the ship.

"You the Captain o' this boat?" demanded Quincy, his eyes flaming green from the rage in his soul. "If you are, put me ashore, or I'll make you sweat!"

"Steady as you go," answered the Captain, quietly. "I'm too big a man to sweat. It's dangerous to make me sweat. What's on your mind?"

"Put us ashore!" yelled Benson, insanely. "Those fellows that hammered us just now said we shipped in this boat. We did not. We were drugged and abducted."

"Whew!" whistled the big skipper, turning his back on them for the moment. Then he turned back and said, "What d'you want?"

"To go ashore and take our prisoner with us. We'll settle between ourselves as to which one gets him."

"Your prisoner? Where is he?"

"That fellow standing there—steering, I suppose," answered Quincy.

The skipper turned toward Rogers. "You a prisoner?" he asked, with the good humor coming of size and self-confidence.

"I'm wanted, Sir," said Rogers, grimly, "in Arizona and in Manitoba. These men are what they say, officers of the law."

"What crime have you committed?"

"None, Sir," answered Rogers; "though I'm indicted in one place for stage robbery and in the other place for murder."

"Well, well!" commented the big man. "You seem to be a dangerous character. What are you doing aboard my ship?"

"These fellows chased me, and I went to a boarding master to get a ship. They followed and were shanghaied with me—though I do not see why he drugged me, Sir; I was willing to ship."

"But did you," demanded the skipper, his voice growing tense and forceful, "rob a stage and kill a man, somewhere in the West?"

"I robbed a stage of what I owned—my own gold-dust. I killed the man who thought I robbed him; but he pulled his gun first, and I shot in self-defense."

"And I've come all the way from Arizona," interrupted Quincy, "to bring this man back for trial. And—I want him!"

"And I've come from Manitoba," added Benson, "where he's wanted for murder."

The skipper turned to Rogers and said calmly, "By your own admission you are a fugitive from justice; hence, entitled to no sympathy from me." Then he turned to the two others and said, "You men put up a plausible story of being shanghaied. If you told it at the dock where I could get two men to replace you, I might put you ashore. As it is, fifty miles outside of Sandy Hook, I can do nothing of the kind. This ship's time is valuable, worth about a hundred dollars a day, and I can't stop to signal and put you aboard an inbound craft. You're signed on my articles—John Quincy and Walter Benson; though I don't know which is which. But the fact is that here you stay, and you work, and earn your grub and what pay I choose to put you on."

"But we did not agree," yelled Quincy. "You have no warrant in law for this procedure."

"I have my articles. I did not ship you, as I was not in the shipping office; but I bargained with a crimp for sixteen men, and he gave me fourteen and you two."

"Well," said Quincy, quietly, "you seem to be in power here, and responsible to no one that we can reach. But I'll tell you that the State of Arizona will swarm about your ears, and that you'll sweat, big as you are!"

"And I'll tell you," spoke up Benson, "that the Secretary of State at Washington will hear from the Governor General at Ottawa!"

"Get out o' this!" exploded the Captain. "Get off the poop, you four-legged farmers! Sweat, will I? All right; but you'll sweat, the both of you, before you see your friends again! Here, Mr. Billings," he roared to the first mate amidships, "and Mr. Snelling! Come up here, and turn these men to!"

The two mates answered and appeared.

"Turn them to," said the Captain, speaking slowly and softly. "Take the starch out of 'em, and make 'em sweat."

The scene that ensued was too painful even for Rogers to witness or describe, except in its salient points. Billings and Snelling pounced upon the two insurgents, struck, buffeted, kicked, and vilified them with foul-mouthed abuse, until they had borne them off the poop, forward along the main deck, and to the vicinity of the forecastle, where the two victims, subdued and quiescent, were willing to dart for cover, when the two mates gave over and went aft.

Rogers at the wheel had watched the scene, at first with a smile; but the smile grew less as he saw the battered men hurled right and left under the blows of the mates, and when at last the punishment was ended his face was serious and resentful. Some criminals do not lose the qualities of forgiveness and mercy. His mood was increased when the big skipper faced him and said:

"A fugitive from justice, are you? Well, I'll see that the Consul at Melbourne gets you. I want no jailbirds in my ship."

Which gave Rogers occasion to think.

Rogers was relieved at one bell (half-past twelve), and went forward to his dinner. As he descended the poop steps he met the big first mate, coming out of the forward companion picking his teeth.

"So," he said to Rogers, "you're a bad man from the West, I hear. Held up a stage and then killed the man you robbed!"

"You've got things wrong, Sir," answered Rogers respectfully.

"None o' your lip!" thundered the officer. "You may be a bad man from the West; but I'm a bad man from the East, and I'm here to take the badness out o' bad men!"

Then, before Rogers could dodge, he launched forth his fist and struck him. The blow knocked him off his feet, and he rose with nose bleeding and eyes closing.

"Just to show you," commented the mate, "that I'm a badder man than you."

Rogers did not answer; in fact, no answer was necessary or wise. He walked forward, and, partly from his half-blindness, partly from his disorganized state of mind, passed to windward of Snelling, the second mate, who was coming aft to dinner. Snelling said nothing in the way of prelude, but crashed his fist on Rogers's already mutilated face, and sent him again to the deck. As Rogers struggled to his feet he said:

"You pass to looward o' me when we meet, or I'll make you jump overboard!"

And again Rogers saw the wisdom of silence and went on to the forecastle.

The watches had not yet been chosen; but half the crew had eaten, and he joined the other half, finding in his clothes bag a new sheath knife and belt, a tin pan, pannikin, and spoon, which articles are always furnished to a shipped man by the boarding masters, no matter how he has been shipped. To his surprise, as he attacked the dinner, he found Quincy and Benson, each with a similar outfit of tinware, toying with the food, and paying no attention to the polyglot discourse of the other men regarding the ship, the mates, and the food. But they glared menacingly at Rogers as he entered.

"This your work, Rogers?" demanded Quincy. "Were you in cahoots with that saloonkeeper?"

"Shut up!" answered Rogers, stabbing at a piece of salt beef with his knife.

"We won't shut up!" said Benson, spooning up pea soup with his brand new tin spoon. "This increases your sentence to the extent of a shorter shrift."

"Go to the devil, the pair of you! I was doped and shanghaied myself, and I've run foul o' the mates, same as you did—and for less reason, too."

"Well, they'll sweat for this, and you, too, Rogers!" said Quincy.

"Shut up! You're up against something now that gunplay doesn't figure in. You're aboard a Yankee hell ship, and you've got to make the best of it."

"I wouldn't if I had my gun," said Quincy, moodily.

"Yes," added Benson, "with a gun I could have my own way."

Rogers straightened back, looked them steadily in their faces, and said, "If you had your guns, what would you do?"

"Make this ship put back and land us," answered Quincy.

"Benson," said Rogers, "what would you do with a gun?"

"Shoot 'em full of holes until they turned this boat back."

"Are you game?" said Rogers. "Understand that you'll be alone. I wouldn't help you; for, having been a sailor, I know what mutiny means in the courts. I'd rather go back with either of you to stand trial than to engage in open mutiny."

"Hang your mutiny!" said Quincy. "We're not sailors; we never agreed to make this voyage. I'm an officer of the law."

"Feel the same way, Benson?" asked Rogers.

"The same. Give me a gun, and I'll make that Captain and his two assistants walk a chalkline."

The rest of the men, engaged with their dinner, had paid no attention to this discourse, and Rogers rose up, reached into his bag, and produced the note he had found there on wakening. "Listen," he said:

BILL ROGERS
"You seem to be a square fellow and up against it. I had to dope you because you would not have signed if you knew the other two would have gone along. But I needed just three men; so I doped you all. You'll find their guns and belts in your bag. Of course, you will know what to do if you get in trouble. Good luck."

"Now," said Rogers, "those guns are not now in my bag, and you can't find them without my say-so; but, if I put you onto them, will you call it off? Will you let up, and go back reporting that I had escaped? If you get ashore by any means, will you take me with you and turn me loose?"

They each looked steadily at Rogers for a moment or two; then Quincy spoke.

"If you can furnish me my gun, Bill, it's all off. I'll resign my job, if necessary; but I won't hunt you any more."

"Benson?" asked Rogers.

"The Canadian Mounted Police and the whole Colonial Government can go hang. Give me a gun, Rogers, and I'll trouble you no more!"

Rogers was about to speak, when the big first mate appeared at the forecastle door, and said in the forceful manner of deep-water mates:

"Turn to. Where's that bloody-minded stage robber? Hey! Here you are! Get aft to the wheel again. You can steer, if you are a murderer."

"All right, Sir," answered Rogers, deferentially, and then, in a whisper to the two, he said, "In my bag, halfway down. Two guns and two belts."

Then Bill Rogers, desperado, outlaw, and fugitive from justice, went to the wheel, and as he steered he smiled again, grimly and painfully, for his nose hurt.

Billings had followed him aft, up on the poop, and to the vicinity of the after companion, where he stood, waiting for the Captain. Snelling, having finished his dinner, had gone forward to oversee the men, all of whom were now on deck and scattering to their various tasks. That is, all but two. Quincy and Benson, each one girdled with a beltful of cartridges, each carrying a heavy revolver, each scowling wickedly, were marching up to Snelling.

"Hands up!" said Quincy, sternly. "Up with 'em and go back to the other end of the boat!"

Involuntarily, it seemed, the second mate obeyed. Up went his hands over his head. Then, remembering that he was second mate, he answered, "What's this? Mutiny! Put them guns down!"

Quincy's gun spat out a red tongue, and Snelling's cap left his head.

"Next time I'll aim lower," said Quincy. "Right about face! March!"

Snelling was impressed. With his hands aloft he wheeled and preceded them to the poop steps, up which he climbed.

But Billings had noticed, and acted. With a shout down the companion to the Captain, he whipped out a pocket revolver and hurried forward in the alley to meet the procession. But he did not use that revolver. Benson took quick aim and fired, and coincident with the report the nickel-plated weapon left his hand, whirling high in air before falling overboard. Billings whinnied in pain, and, rubbing his benumbed hand, backed aft before the advancing Snelling.

Then, up the companion on a run, came the Captain, a fat cigar in his mouth and a look of wonder and astonishment on his face. Benson and Quincy were now in the alley, and again a pistol spoke—Quincy's, this time—and the fat cigar left the Captain's mouth in two pieces.

"Hands up, all three of you," yelled Quincy, "or we'll shoot to kill! Found out, haven't you, that we can shoot—some? That's our trade. Up with your hands!"

Both Captain and mate raised their hands, but the former protested. "This is mutiny, you scoundrels! D'you know the penalty? Ten years!"

"It won't be ten minutes," answered Quincy. "Call it what you like, mutiny, burglary, or pistol practice. But I'll tell you what it sure will be, if you don't come to time. It'll be a pig killing, and justifiable manslaughter in the courts. I know something about law, and I've got you for abduction. A man abducted has a right to defend himself, and I'll kill you if you don't head this boat for land and put us ashore."

"Yes," added Benson, "and we'll take our prisoner with us, too!"

"Sure," said Quincy. "Bill Rogers goes, too. Come, now, what do you say?"

"I say, by Gawd," roared the Captain, red in the face with rage and the strain on his muscles, "that I won't! If this ship goes back, you'll take her back yourself, with me and my mates under duress. It's ruinous to agree to such a proposition. I'd lose this ship and never get another."

"Very well," said Quincy, quietly. "Then we'll put you fellows under arrest. And if you resist we'll shoot you to pieces. Rogers," he turned to the smiling helmsman, "can you steer this boat back to the United States?"

"I can't find New York," answered Rogers; "but the United States is due west."

"Can you steer due west?"

"Yes; but the yards must be braced. The wind is hauling to the north, and we could make a fair wind of it."

"Can you attend to this—bracing of the yards?"

"Yes. I've been second mate."

"Right, Benson, go through them all and take away their guns, if they have any!" Then he raised his voice and called forward to the men, who had stopped work and were watching curiously the strange scene on the poop. "One of you fellows get a piece of small rope cord. Bring it up here and tie these fellows' hands behind their backs."

While Benson searched the pockets of the trio—finding no weapons, however—a man had secured a ball of spun yarn from the booby hatch and ran up the poop steps with it. Then, under the influence of those long, blue tubes, the Captain and the two mates lay down on their faces, while the sailor securely bound their wrists behind them.

"Now, then," said Quincy, "you're in command, Rogers. We'll police this boat, and make these men obey all your orders."

"Take the wheel here!" said Rogers to the sailor. "Stand by to wear ship!" Then he mounted the cabin, and emitted a sailorly yell to the crew. "All hands down from aloft! Weather main and lee crowjack braces!"

IN THE DAWN OF THE following morning some early rising fishermen of the Jersey coast saw a black ship with all canvas set resting quietly on the sands about two hundred yards from the beach, a white boat, empty of everything but oars, hauled out above high-water mark, and on boarding the ship they found and released three chilled, hungry, and angry men from the lazaret. But not a sign of her crew did they see.

SHOVELS AND BRICKS

M r. John Murphy, boarding master, was on bad terms with himself. He had been kicked off the poop-deck of Captain Williams's big ship, the *Albatross*, lying off Tompkinsville, waiting to dock, thence to the gangway, and from there shoved, struck in the face, and further kicked and maltreated until he had flopped into the boat at the foot of the steps. Williams was a six-footer, a graduate "bucko" now in charge of this big skysail-yarder, and he had resented Murphy's appearance on board with whisky and kind words for his men before he was through with them. Not caring to dock his ship with the help of riggers at five dollars a day, he had called Murphy aft, lectured him on the ethics and proprieties of seafaring, and then had punished him for an indiscreet reference to the rights of boarding masters who must needs solicit boarders in order to make a living. All that Murphy could do under the circumstances was to shout up from the boat his defiance of Captain Williams, and a threat to prevent his getting a new crew when ready to sail—which was clearly within his power as a member of the Association of Boarding and Shipping Masters. But Williams, red-bearded, angry-faced, and victorious, replied with injunctions to descend to the infernal regions and remain there, and Murphy pulled ashore and took the boat to New York, bent upon vengeance.

At the door of his boarding-house in Front Street he met Hennesey, his runner. Hennesey was a small man, sly, shrewd, and persuasive, and so far had given satisfaction in the difficult business of soliciting incoming crews to board at Murphy's house instead of the Sailors' Home, the Provident Seamen's Mission, and other like institutions. But Murphy's mood was strong upon him, and he asked, peremptorily:

"Well, what did ye git?"

"Nothin'; the Mission launch wuz on hand and the bunch wint in a body."

"Dom yer soul, what do I pay ye fur, anyhow?" stormed Murphy. "Are ye no good? Tell me thot. Are ye no good at all? What are ye takin' my money fur?"

"To git sailors to come to yer house on commission," retorted Hennesey, hotly; "an' fur fear I'd be makin' too much, ye sind me to a bloody coaster, whose min are in the union, while you go down to the *Albatross*, in from deep water."

"I got no wan from the *Albatross*."

"No fault o' yours or mine. I'd ha' got 'em."

"None o' yer shlack."

"To hill wi' ye."

"Ye're discharged. Come in an' I'll pay ye off."

"Right ye are. From this on I'll work fur mesilf and git your business, ye skin."

Hennesey's estimate of Murphy was not far wrong, though it might also apply to himself. The profits of a sailors' boarding-house depend not upon the cash paid in by men with money, who choose their own ship and come and go as they please, but upon the advance or allotment of pay which the law allows to deep-water seamen in order that they may purchase an outfit of clothing before sailing. To get this allotment, Murphy and others of his kind would take in and feed any penniless sailor long enough to run up an inflated bill for board, money lent, and clothing, then find him a ship and walk him to the shipping-office, more or less drugged or drunk. Here the penniless sailor dared not, even if suspicious, contest the claim, for, should he do so, he would find himself not only out of a ship, but out of a boarding-house; so he would sign away his allotment, and go aboard with what clothing his benefactor had allowed him. As deep-water men on shore are invariably drunk, drugged, or penniless, the boarding-masters, to whom the skippers must apply for men, easily control the situation. And, as machinery for such control, nearly all boarding-houses have the front ground floor divided into barroom and clothing-store, while in the rear is the dining-room and upstairs the bedrooms, each with as many beds as there is room for. Thus, a man may be housed, fed, clothed, drugged, and shipped from the same address. The remedy for this has no place in this story.

A boarding-master, or crimp, without the machinery, becomes a shipping-master, a go-between between the skipper and the boarding-master, whose income is the blood-money paid by skippers for men. Murphy, strolling along South Street a few days later, saw a new sign over a doorway—Timothy Hennesey, Shipping-Master. He ascended the wooden stairs, and in a dingy room with one desk and chair found his former aid.

"Well, what the hill is this, Hennesey—tryin' to take the brid out of honest min's mouths?"

"I've me livin' to make, Murphy, an' I'm a-doin' it. I got the crew of the *Albatross*."

"An' what did ye do wid 'em?"

"Put 'em wid Stillman, over beyant. Ye might ha' had 'em had ye played fair."

Stillman was Murphy's most important rival, and the news did not cheer him. He glared darkly at Hennesey.

"An' I've got the shippin' o' Williams's new crew whin he sails," continued Hennesey, "an' I'll not go to you for 'em, Murphy."

"Ye'll not?" responded Murphy, luridly. "After all the wark I've given ye."

"I'll not. I told ye I'd git yer business, an' I'll do it."

Murphy's fist shot out and Hennesey went down. Arising with bleeding nose, he shook his small fist at his chuckling assailant passing sidewise out of his door.

"I'll not forgit thot, John Murphy," he spluttered.

"I don't want ye to. Remember it while ye live; an' there's more where thot cum from, too, ye scab."

At a meeting of the brotherhood that evening, Murphy posted the name of Timothy Hennesey, scab, and Captain Williams, outlaw; then, somewhat easier in his mind, took account of the immediate business situation. It was bad; he had three cash boarders, of no use when their money was gone, as they signed in coasters, and there was but one ship in port, the *Albatross*, and none expected for a fortnight. So, leaving orders with his wife to watch the cash register in the bar, and to evict the boarders when they asked for trust, he took the train for Chicago, where lived a prosperous brother, for whom he had a sincere regard, and to whom he owed a long-promised visit. Brother Mike welcomed him, and under the softening influence of brotherly love he forgave Hennesey, but not Williams. It is so much easier to warm toward a fellow man you have punched than toward one who has punched you.

Mike took John down to his coal-docks, with which he was amassing a fortune, and explained their workings. A schooner lay at one, and his gang was unloading her. It was a cold day in November, and their warm overcoats felt none too warm; yet down in the hold of the schooner were men bare to the waist, black as negroes with coal dust, save where the perspiration cleared white channels as it ran down their backs and breasts—keeping themselves warm with the violence of their exertions. There were two to each of the three hatches; and there were six others on the dock runway, wheeling the coal away; they had nearly unloaded the schooner, having cleared away the coal directly under the hatch, and were now loading their buckets at the two piles farther back, between the hatches. These buckets stood as high as their waists, and held, according to Brother Mike, five hundred pounds when full. But a man, having filled it to the brim, would seize the bale and drag it along the flooring to the hatch, unhook a descending bucket, hook on the full one, sing out an inarticulate cry, and drag the empty back to the coal to be filled in its turn—all with a never-lessening display of extravagant muscular force.

"Heavens! what wark!" said John, as they peered down the hatch. "An' how long do they kape this up?"

"Tin hours a day, and not a minute longer," answered Mike; "that is, barrin' fifteen minutes at tin in the mornin' and three in the afternoon, whin they knock off for a bite and a drink up at me place on the corner. They go up and ate up me free lunch and soak in about a pint of whisky at one drink."

"The divil! and don't it kill thim?"

"Naw. They come back and sweat it out. They couldn't wurruk like this widout it."

"It's great work, Mike. Look at the devilopment. Did ye iver see a prize-fighter with such muscles?"

"A prize-fighter!" said Mike. "Jawn Murphy, luk at them. They're all sizes, big and little, in my two gangs; but give the littlest a month's trainin' in the science o' boxin' and he'd lick any heavyweight in the wurruld. Ye see, ye simply can't hurt 'em."

"Can't hurt 'em?"

"Ye can't hurt 'em. They're not human. They're wild beasts. They come from the hills and bogs of Limerick and Galway, and they can't speak the language, but call themselves Irishmin. Well, Jawn, they're Irish, mebbe, as the American Injun's an American; but they're not like you and me, dacent min from Dublin."

"But if they can't speak the language, how do ye git on wid 'em?"

"Once in a while, when they're cool and tranquil, I get on to a word or two, but usually I fall back on moral suasion and the sign language."

"Moral suasion?"

"I swear at 'em. And thin, whin that fails, I use the sign language. That's good in talkin' to any foreigner, Jawn."

"But what is it, the sign language?"

"A brick. See this, Jawn?" Mike held up one side of his coat, and John felt of an oblong protuberance in the right-hand pocket. "I carry a brick at all times, Jawn, for it's the only thing that appeals to their sinsibilities. I used to carry a club, but it didn't wurruk; they'd get back at me wid their shovels, and it's domned inconvanient, Jawn, to be sliced up wid a shovel. So, I carry a brick."

"Do they git that way often?"

"Yis; it's their natural condition. They'd rather fight than ate, and I don't dare hire a man from another county in one gang, for fear they'll kill him; so this is the Galway gang, and up the dock a bit is the Limerick gang, twilve min to each. They're all alike, but think they're different, so I have to be careful. But, while they'd rather fight than ate, they'd rather wurruk than fight, and that's where I come in. I kape 'em apart, and stir up their jealousy. Each gang 'll wurruk like hill to bate the other."

"And what do ye pay thim?"

"By the job. They stick to factory hours, and won't wurruk overtime, but at tin hours a day they make about eight dollars."

"The divil! But that's big pay."

"Yis; but I have to pay it, for no other class o' min can do the wurruk. Why, it 'ud kill an American or a Dootchman!"

"They must have money saved up."

"All that they don't spind at me bar up on the corner. They have to save some, for in the nature o' things I can't git it all back. And they're all goin' back to the old sod whin navigation closes—in about two weeks. This'll be about their last job."

"They'll come to New York and take passage, I suppose."

"Yis; and I'll have to buy their tickets and ship thim. They don't know much about American money, and wid a new man I have to pay him in English money at first, until he finds it's no good; thin I exchange at a discount."

"Fine, Mike; ye'll be rich before long."

"That I will, if the supply of bog-trottin' savages holds out."

At this juncture one of the men in the hold lifted his sooty countenance and, with the vehemence of a lunatic, delivered this:

"Whythilldonye'veaharseut'lldothwark?"

"Dry up," said Mike, pulling the brick from his pocket. "Dry up or I'll hurt yer feelin's."

The man shrank back out of sight, and Mike put the brick back in his pocket.

"What did he say?" queried John.

"He objicts to the speed o' the harse on the dock. He can fill buckets, ye see, faster than the harse can h'ist 'em. That's what ails him."

"And he's afraid o' the brick?"

"Yis; but o' nothin' else. Thim fellers don't fear a gun, so I don't carry one. Why, a while back, there was a bad time at the corner whin the two gangs got mixed up, and the police cum down. They used their guns, but—hill! the bullets just punctured their skins, and they picked thim out wid their fingers and wint for the coppers and done thim up. I tell ye, Jawn, that a wild Irishman, frish from the bogs and the hills, can outwork, outfight, and outeat any man alive."

"Outeat?"

"I give thim mate three times a day. If it wuzn't for the profits o' the bar, it wud brek me. And, say, Jawn, they can't say 'mate' whin they ask for more. They say 'mate.'"

"'Mate'? And can't they say 'mate,' whin they ate it so much?"

"No, Jawn, they sing out for mate. It's no use; they can't spake the language, and it's no use t'achin' thim. They're good min to wurruk—all bone and sole leather, but ye can't refine thim."

"You can't, Mike, but I kin."

"How, ye skeptic? Luk at 'em. Scratch 'em, and they won't bleed. Shoot 'em, and they'll pick out the bullets and paste ye wid 'em. Reason wid 'em, and they'll insult ye. Refine 'em, Jawn! Ye're crazy. Luk at thot felly down there under the hatch. He's here on his weddin' trip, but he lift his wife behind in the old country."

"That makes no difference," answered John, ruminatively; "I can refine 'em. Make sure, Mike, that whin they come to New York they come to my house in Front Street. I'll feed 'em mate three times a day again' the time they take the ship for the old sod. I'll be good to thim, Mike. Send thim to me."

"Ay, John, I will thot. But ye'll nade to square yerself wid yer butcher in advance if ye think to feed thim wolfs. They're hungry and they're thirsty be nature."

"Never mind. Send thim on, both factions. I'll take care o' thim. They're a fine lot o' min, and I'll be good to 'em."

John verified Mike's description of them when they met, both gangs, at their afternoon recess in Mike's barroom. They conversed in shouts and whoops, uttering words that, while they bore a slight resemblance to English, were in the main unintelligible. Murphy endeavored to find those whose sole-leather flesh had stopped a bullet, but could not.

However, digging his fingers into the breasts and shoulders of a few of the quietest convinced him that the story could not be far wrong. The stiffened muscles felt like bones.

He treated them all, and was glad, when he saw them drink, that he had not promised them free whisky at his house; but he reiterated his promise of "mate" three times a day, and secured their promise to board at his house while waiting for sailing-day. This done, he finished his visit and returned to New York.

His first task was to estimate the business situation; it was the same, except that his boarders had gone at the request of Mrs. Murphy. This was good, almost as good as the news that Williams's old crew had scattered and that there was not a deep-water man in port to aid Hennesey in his first job in the shipping business. He cautiously hunted for Hennesey, meeting him by accident, as he said, in the street at daytime, safe from possible bricks or clubs coming out of the dark.

"And how are ye, Tim?" he said, exuberantly, as he extended his hand.

"So so," answered Hennesey, ignoring the greeting and eying his late employer suspiciously. "And how is it wid you?"

"Fine, Hennesey, fine. In a week I'll have as fine a crew of min in me house as iver ye laid eyes on. Lake sailors, every wan o' thim. And I'll be after havin' to find thim a ship."

"That's easier than to find the min," said Hennesey, still watching for a sudden demonstration of Murphy's fist. "I'll be goin' to Philadelphy, I think, or Boston."

"And it'll cost ye a hundred, Hennesey. I've done it. It takes a cool hundred to bring a crew on from either port. Don't be a fule, Hennesey. I'm domned sorry I slugged ye. I wuz put out, ye see, but I felt bad about it nixt day. I can't deal wid Williams, the dog, but I can wid you, and you can wid him."

"Speak up. What do ye want, John Murphy?"

"That we git together, Hennesey, for our mutual advantage. Give up this idee of gittin' me business away from me. Ye can't do it. I'm too well established, and the only skipper I've blacklisted is Williams, and he's all ye've got."

"What do I git out of it?"

"Ye git your blood-money from Williams, widout huntin' up yer min. I git the allotment agin' the expense I'm put to in feedin' thim. The regular thing, except thot ye make more than ye would as a runner—

only ye've got to muster 'em into the shippin'-office and sign 'em. I can't appear. Williams might be there, and cold-deck the deal."

"Murphy, gimme me job back and I'm wid ye. But I want me priveleges—a drink whin I nade it, and access to the bar for me frinds."

"Right, Hennesey; let bygones be bygones. Put this job through as shippin'-master, and thin go on wid me as runner. Shake hands."

They shook, Murphy joyous and forgiving, Hennesey cold, suspicious, and unforgiving. A handshake is a poor auditing of a fist blow.

"Whin does Williams want his min?" asked Murphy.

"In two weeks, about. Twinty-four able seamen."

"Thot's good. I'll have to feed 'em a week, and thot's dead loss; but I'll be contint; yes, I'll be contint, Hennesey, if I can furnish Williams wid the right kind of a crew, God d—bliss him!"

"Ye're gittin' religion, are ye not?" asked Hennesey. "I heard he slugged ye around decks and bundled ye down into yer boat.'"

"Yes"—and Murphy's eyes shone—"but thot's all past, Hennesey. I'm not the man to hold a grudge. Ye know thot."

"But I am," muttered Hennesey, as they parted.

And thus did Murphy plan his dark vengeance upon Captain Williams. It went through without a hitch; the twenty-four wild men from Galway and Limerick, shipped on by Brother Mike, arrived at Murphy's house in a few days, and were housed and fed—"mate" with every meal—to the scandal of Mrs. Murphy, who averred that she "niver seed such min."

"Fur they have no table manners, John," she said. "What's the use givin' thim knives and forks, whin they don't know how to use thim? Foor o' thim cut their mouths."

"Niver mind, Norah," said Murphy, kindly. "Give thim spoons; for a spoon is like a shovel, ye know, and they're accustomed to shovels. And give 'em bafe stew and mashed praties."

"I'll give 'em rat pizen, if I have to sarve 'em much longer," responded the good lady. "I was a silf-respictin' woman before I married you, John Murphy, and didn't have to consort wid lunatics."

"Niver mind, Norah," answered Murphy, soothingly. "I'll be rid o' thim in a few days, and ye'll have a new driss out o' the proceeds."

The proceeds were secured. Murphy collected a week's board in advance from each, and induced them to deposit their money with him for safe-keeping. Then he got them drunk on his tried and true whisky, and kept them so; then he collected ten dollars from each for a ticket to Queenstown on the ship which would sail in a few days; and then he audited an account for each, charging them with money advanced as they asked for it. As he always trebled the amount that they asked for, and as they were too drunk and befuddled to contest the word of so good and kind a man, Murphy had a tidy sum due him when the allotments were signed.

This happened in due time and form. Captain. Williams, knowing by experience that no crew would sign with him if he showed himself, remained away from the shipping-office and took his ship down to the Horseshoe with the help of his two mates, cook, steward, and a tug, leaving his articles in the care of Hennesey, and trusting to him to sign the crew and bring them down in the tug that would tow him out past the light-ship.

Hennesey did his part. As the *Albatross* was bound for Liverpool *viâ* Queenstown in ballast, there was only part deception in walking the twenty-four to the shipping-office to sign their names (or marks) on the ship's articles, which they cheerfully did, under the impression that it was a necessary matter of form connected with their purchase of tickets; and while the Shipping Commissioner marveled somewhat at the hilarity and the ingenuous self-assertiveness of this crew of sailormen, he forebore to express himself, and left the matter to Captain Williams and Providence. So, with all their allotment or advance signed away to Murphy against the entertainment they had received, and with their pockets depleted from their sublime trust in Murphy's bookkeeping, they went back to the boarding-house, the signed slaves of Bucko Bill Williams, a man they had not met.

It was a wild night, that last night in the boarding-house. The Galways and the Limericks got to fighting, and only Murphy's "pull" with the police prevented a raid. Mrs. Murphy quit the scene early in the evening, going back to her mother with unkind comments on the company that Murphy kept, and Murphy, with a brick in his pocket, and sometimes in his hand, was busy each minute in settling a dispute between this man and that. At last he and Hennesey agreed that it was time to quiet them; so Hennesey, behind the bar, filled twenty-four pint flasks, each with a moderate addition of "knockout drops," and with much flourish of oratory brought the crowd up to the bar for a last drink and the presentation of the flasks. The drinks were also seasoned, and soon Murphy and Hennesey had a long hour's work in lifting the twenty-four able seamen up to the bedrooms, to sleep until the express wagons came to take them and their dunnage to the tug. They came at ten o'clock, and the unconscious men were carried down with their grips and boxes, and loaded in like so many bags of potatoes.

"It's done, Hennesey," said Murphy, as, perspiring and fatigued, he fetched back into the barroom. "Now, Hennesey, let's you and me have a drink, and we'll drink to the health and the happiness of Bucko Bill Williams, the dog."

"Right," said Hennesey, going behind the bar and bringing out the bottle and the glasses; "but we'll need to hurry, Murphy, for I've got to go down wid the tug, ye know." As he spoke he passed his hand over the glass he had placed for Murphy, and Murphy, glancing out through the door at the departing express wagons, did not see.

But Hennesey had another express wagon in reserve, and when Murphy sagged down and sought the nearest chair and table, too stupefied to even wonder at his sleepiness, Hennesey called this wagon from the corner and, with the help of the driver, bundled Murphy into it, climbed in himself, and rode down to the dock and the waiting tug.

It was broad daylight when Murphy woke, in a forecastle bunk, with a dull, dragging pain in his head which he knew from experience was the after effects of a drug. He rolled out, noticing that each bunk held a sleeping man, and, examining a few, recognized his boarders. The plan had succeeded, but why was he there? Then he remembered that last drink, and calling down silent curses upon Hennesey, went out on deck.

The big ship was plowing along before the wind with not a rag set except the foretopmast-staysail and jib. Amidships was a man coiling up ropes, at the wheel was another man, and pacing the top of the after-house was Captain Williams, red-bearded, red-eyed, and truculent of gesture and expression. These three bore marks of hard usage, bruises, black eyes, swollen noses, and contusions. Murphy climbed the forecastle deck and looked astern. The land was a thin line of blue on the horizon.

He descended and went aft. The man coiling ropes, whom Murphy learned later was the first mate, looked furtively at him as he passed, and turned in his tracks so as not to show him his back. Murphy judged that he was nervous over something that had happened—something connected with his injuries. Climbing the poop steps, he was stopped by Captain Williams, who descended from the house and faced him.

"Well, Murphy, what the hell are *you* doing here? Are you in on this deal?"

"What deal, Captain?" asked Murphy, meekly, for it was no place for self-respect.

"This deal I got from your discharged runner, Hennesey. I only dealt with the fellow because he told me he had quit you. And look at what he gave me for a crew—twenty-four wild Micks that, let alone the ropes, can't speak English or understand it. Are you a party to this trick, Murphy?"

"I'm not," declared Murphy, stoutly. "The domned villain doped me last night, and must ha' put me aboard wid the crew he shipped for you. What for, I don't know. He had yer full count, as he told me."

"Guess you're the man he hoisted up himself, saying you were willing to work your passage without pay. So I let you come and sleep it off."

"He did!" stormed Murphy, "the dirty, ungrateful dog! I took him in and gave him wark, and I took him back after I'd discharged him. And now I git this! O' course, Captain, ye'll put me aboard the first ship me meet bound in."

"Not much, I won't. If you took Hennesey back you're in on this deal."

"I'm not in it. Where's Hennesey now, Captain Williams?"

"Went back in the tug, I suppose. He didn't stop to get his receipt signed for the men he delivered. So, he gets no money for this kind of a crew. They're not sailors, and he loses. Moreover, Murphy, you lose. Hennesey brought me the articles, and every man Jack o' them signed his allotment over to you as favored creditor. That means that Hennesey got this bunch out of your house. As they're not sailors, I mean to disrate them to boys at five dollars a month. That's the allotment you get, if you care to sue for it; but I told the tug captain to notify the owners to pay no allotment notes."

"Ye did?" spluttered Murphy. "Well, Williams, I'll sue, don't ye fear. I'll sue."

"That's as may be," said Williams, coldly. "Meanwhile, you'll sing small, do what you're told, and work your passage; and any time that you forget where you are, call on me and I'll tell you."

"Ye want me to wark me passage, do ye? And what'll I do? It's gone twinty years since I've been to sea. I can't go aloft, wi' the fat on me."

"I see," said the skipper, seriously, "that your displacement is more than your dimensions call for. Can you boss that bunch of Kollkenny cats?"

MORGAN ROBERTSON

"I can," said Murphy, mournfully and hopelessly, "if ye'll do yer share. Give me a brick to carry in me pocket, and I'll make 'em wark. They're rival factions from Limerick and Galway, and each side'll wark like hill to bate the other. I can stir 'em up to this, but I can't control thim widout a brick."

"All right. Dig a brick out of the galley floor. Anything in reason to get sail on this ship. The topsails 'll do till they learn."

"All right, Captain," said Murphy, meekly. "I'm in for it, and I've got to make the best of it. Shall I rouse 'em out now?"

"No; they're no good till sober. But steal their bottles before they wake. You fitted them out with some pretty strong stuff, I take it. They wakened at daylight, just as the tug came, mobbed the faces off me and the two mates, and only manned the windlass at last when I told them it made the boat go. Well, I can understand the rivalry. They took sides, each gang together, and hove on the brakes, faster than I ever saw a windlass go round before. When they'd got the anchor apeak and the mate told them to stop it made no difference. They hove the anchor up to the hawse-pipes, and would have parted the chain if it had been weaker. Then they took another drink out of their bottles and went to sleep. The tug pushed us out past the light-ship and left us. So, here we are."

"Well, Captain," said the subdued Murphy, "I'll git me brick, and let me ask ye. If ye've any shovels lyin' loose, stow 'em away. A shovel is a deadly weapon in the hands o' wan o' these fellys."

Murphy went forward to the galley, and soon had pried out a solid, well-preserved brick from under the stove in the galley floor, against the aggrieved protest of the Chinese cook.

"Dry up, ye Chink," said Murphy. "Tell me, though, what's the bill o' fare for the forecastle. Mate three times a day?"

"Meat foul timey one week," answered the Chinaman.

"God help ye, doctor!" said Murphy, kindly. "Kape well widin yer galley, and have a carvin'-knife sharp; or better still, dig out another brick for yersilf. I've troubles o' me own."

Stepping out of the galley, Murphy met Hennesey emerging from the port forecastle door.

"Well, ye rakin's o' Newgate, and what are *you* doin' here?" he demanded, fiercely. "Ye doped me successfully, Hennesey, and here I am wid our account unsettled. But what brings *you* here?"

"Kape yer hands off me, John Murphy, and I'll tell ye. The dope in the bottles was too strong for me, but not for thim. When they wakened at daylight they found me among 'em with the tug alongside, and insisted that I drink wid thim 'fore goin' aboard the tug."

"And ye did?"

"I did. They had their fingers at me throat, Murphy. So I drank. I git this for tryin' to help you out in your schemes, John Murphy."

"And I git this for not watchin' you, Tim Hennesey. Gwan aft; the old man 'll make ye a bosun like me; then come forrard and git yerself a brick agin' the time whin they wake up. Our lives are in danger whin they find out they've got to wark a wind-jammer across to the old sod. We'll settle our private account later on."

Murphy accompanied Hennesey aft and listened to his explanations to Captain Williams. They were glib and apologetic.

"I didn't know," he said, "that they weren't sailormin. And they were the only min in port, and Murphy had 'em; so I shipped 'em."

"Exactly," answered the captain, coldly; "and they shipped you. You two fellows are caught in the plant you prepared for me, and you've got to stand for it. Ever been to sea, Hennesey?"

"Tin years, Captain. I'm an able seaman, though not a heavy man."

"Heavy enough. Get a brick out of the galley, and I'll make you a bosun without pay. You two will make those tarriers work. Come aft to the wheel, the pair of you. Mr. Baker"—this to the man coiling ropes, who dropped his task and followed—"Mr. Baker," said the captain, "and Mr. Sharp"—he turned to the man at the wheel—"these two men have some influence over the crew, and I've made them acting bosuns. They've been to sea, and their part is to loose canvas and put ropes into the hands of the others. Your part is to see that they do it."

The two officers turned their swollen faces toward Murphy and Hennesey, and inspected them through closed and blackened eyelids. Then they nodded, and the introduction was complete.

"Come, Hennesey," said Murphy, briskly, now that the situation was defined. "We'll be gettin' a brick for ye, and wan each for the skipper and the mates. We'll need 'em. Thin we'll go through 'em for the dope, and then we'll loose the canvas."

For this short run across the Atlantic Captain Williams had shipped neither carpenter, sailmaker, nor boatswains, he and his two mates, a weakling steward and the Chinese cook representing the afterguard until the advent of Murphy and Hennesey. To properly equip this afterguard, Murphy pried out six more bricks from under the galley stove, solemnly distributed them with instructions as to their use, and then he and Hennesey replevined the half-empty bottles from the sleepers, an easy task for such skilled craftsmen.

About noon the twenty-four awakened and clamored for their dinner. It was served, and as it contained meat in plenty it was satisfactory; then, smoking their clay pipes, they mustered on deck and, more or less unconsciously, divided into two parts, the Galways separate from the Limericks.

"Loose the foretopsail, Hennesey," said Murphy, as he looked at them. "Overhaul the gear and stop it so ye can come down. Thin take the halyards to the fo'c'stle capstan. I'll take the main."

The first mate was content to remain out of the proceedings for the present. Murphy and Hennesey went aloft, performed their part, and came down; then, when the two falls of the halyards were led to the two capstans, Murphy, with his hand in his pocket and his heart in his mouth, went among them.

"I want," he said, sourly, "twilve good min, but I don't know that I can git them. Ye're a lot o' bog-trotters that don't know enough to heave on a capstan."

"The hill we don't!" uttered a Galway man close to him.

"We l'arned thot in Checa-a-go."

"Ye mane," said Murphy, "that the Limerick boys *tried* to l'arn, but they couldn't. The wark's too hard."

"Fwat's too ha-a-rd?" answered the Galway. "Ye domned murderer, fwat's too hard? D'y' think we can't wurruk?"

"D'ye think ye *can* wark?" said Murphy. "Thin git at that capstan, you Galway min. And git busy, quick, or I'll give the job to the Limerick boys. They're passably good min, I think."

"To hill wi' thim! Hurrah, here, b'ys. C'm'an and pull the mon's rope. Who says we can't wurruk?"

They joyously and enthusiastically surrounded the forecastle capstan, shipped the brakes, and began to heave, with black looks at the envious Limericks, to whom Murphy now addressed himself.

"Are yez lookin' for wark?" he demanded.

"Yis," they chorused.

"Man that 'midship capstan, thin. Beat these Galway sogers and I'll give ye wark right along."

With whoops and shouts they flocked to the capstan amidships, and began to compete, shoving on the bars, cheering and encouraging each other and deriding those on the forecastle deck, who responded. It was a tie; the Galways had about a minute start, but the Limericks finished only a minute behind. Murphy and Hennesey nippered the falls at the pinrail, and belayed when they slacked.

"It goes, Hennesey," said Murphy, wiping the perspiration from his brow. "By puttin' wan gang agin' the other, maybe we won't need to show the bricks."

"Yes," replied Hennesey, "that's all right; but I oncet heard an old, wise skipper say that any farmer can make sail, but it takes a sailor to take it in. What'll we do if it comes on to blow?"

"That's the least o' your troubles, and mine, Tim Hennesey. Put yer trust in Jasus and loose that mizzentopsail, while I get 'em to steady the braces."

But the demoralized first mate had so far aroused himself as to attend to the loosing of the mizzen topsail and topgallant sail; so Murphy with a little cajolery and ridicule induced the crew to sheet home and tauten the braces, then mustered them aft to the mizzentopsail halyards and asked them if they could, the whole lazy two dozen of them, masthead that yard by hand, without the aid of the capstan. They noisily averred that they could, and they did, nearly parting the halyards when the yard could go no higher. The chain-sheets they could not break, hard as they tried.

"It's not according to seamanship, Hennesey," said Murphy, "to man yer halyards before ye sheet home; but—any way at all with this bunch. Now git up to the foreto'gallant and the royal, while I take the main. The poor mate's done his stunt on the mizzen."

And so, by doing the seamanly work themselves and putting ropes into the hands of the crew, the mate and the two boatswains got sail on the ship, even to the jib-topsail and the mainroyal staysail. Captain Williams discreetly remained in the background, only asserting himself once, when he knocked an Irishman off the poop. For this indiscretion he was menaced by violent death, and only saved himself by an appeal to Murphy, respect for whose diplomacy was fast overcoming Captain Williams's dislike of him.

"What do ye think?" stormed Murphy, as he faced the angry men at the break of the poop. "Whin ye came over in the steamer did they allow ye up in the bridge, or aft o' the engine-room hatch? Stay forrard where ye belong, and don't git presumptions, just 'cause ye've been a year in a free country. Yer goin' back to Ireland now, to eat praties and drink water. There's no whisky on this boat, and no mate three times a day. No mate, d'ye understand?"

"No mate!" they vociferated. "No whusky!"

"No, ye bundle o' bad min, no whisky. Ye've drunk up what ye had, and that was in America. Yer not in America now, and ye'll git no whisky, nor mate, barrin' four times a week."

"We paid fur ut," they declaimed. "How kin a mon wurruk widout it?"

"Ye *can* wark widout it and ye will. Ye'll pull ropes as I tell you, and as ye l'arn ye'll steer the boat in yer turn."

"We'll shteer, will we?"

"Yes, ye'll steer, straight for old Ireland and praties."

"Hurrah! We'll git to the ould sod, will we?"

"Yes, but ye'll do it yerselves, mind ye. No kicks, no scraps. Ye'll do as yer told, and pull ropes, and wark."

"We'll wurruk," they declared, noisily. "It's not the loikes o' you th't'll foind the wurruk we can't do, nayther."

"We'll see," said Murphy, nodding his head portentously.

"Meanwhile, take yerself away from this end o' the boat, and stay away from it; and don't ye ever raise yer hands agin' any man that lives in this end o' the boat, or things'll happen to ye. Now git."

He drew forth the brick, and they left his vicinity.

"Captain Williams," said Murphy, solemnly, "that was a close call. If ye'll take my advice, Captain, ye won't lay hands on 'em."

"Why?" answered the skipper. "Do you think I'm going to have them trooping around my cabin?"

"No, not at all; but show 'em the brick, only don't use it, or they'll throw it back. And don't make any gun-play, for they don't know what it means, and it's no good, for ye can't shoot into thim. They're that hard that they'll turn a bullet, I'm told."

"Possibly," said the captain, looking at his hand. "I hurt myself when I hit him. Well, Murphy, all right, if you can control them. I can see that I might have to shoot them all if I shot one, and that wouldn't do."

"No, of course not, sir. I'll l'arn a few of them to steer, and the mates'll be rid of it."

So, under these conditions they worked the ship across the western ocean. By tact and "sign language" Murphy induced them to stand their tricks at the wheel; but they would stand no tutelage, and steered in their own way—a zizzag track over the sea. Another limitation which they imposed upon their usefulness was their emphatic refusal to stand watch, though from inward impulse they divided themselves into watches. They would work factory hours, or not at all, so Captain Williams had to be content with the loss of most of his light sails before the passage was half over. For a sudden increase of wind at night would occasionally prove too much for Murphy or Hennesey, with the mate on watch. As for going aloft, day or night, their case was too hopeless, even for the optimistic Murphy, even had they been willing to leave the deck—which, most decidedly, they were not.

Even so, this passage might have reached a successful termination, the homeward-bound Irishmen safely landed at Queenstown, and the others graduated in a much-needed schooling in the doctrine of the brotherhood of man; but Captain Williams, against Murphy's urgent and earnest plea for more meat on the forecastle menu, persisted in sticking to the original diet. The *Albatross* was a "full-and-plenty" ship—that is, one in which, with the supposed consent of the crew, the government scale was discarded in favor of one containing more vegetables and less meat. But these men knew nothing of this, or the reasons for it; and while believing that there was no whisky in the ship, they had accepted this deprivation, they were firmly assured that there was plenty of meat; so day by day their discontent grew, until by the time the ship had reached soundings they were ripe for open revolt. And it was the small, weakling steward that brought it about.

The passage had been good for all except this steward. It had brought to Captain Williams and his two mates, now recovered in mind and body from the first friction, the unspoken but fixed conception that there were men in the world not afraid of them. It had reduced Murphy's fat, and his resentment against Hennesey and Captain Williams. It had increased Hennesey's respect for Murphy and lessened his respect for himself; for without Murphy's moral support he could not have done his part. It had eliminated the alcohol from the veins and the brains of the twenty-four wild men, and lessened the propensity to kill at the same time that it lessened their fear of a brick. It had lessened the sublime, ages-old contempt for white men that the Chinese cook shared with his countrymen, and which simply *had* to yield to the fear of death inspired by three or four frenzied Irish faces at the galley door, their owners demanding "mate." But the small steward, busy with his cabin dishes, his cabin carpets, only visiting the galley to obtain the cabin meals, had seen nothing, felt nothing, and learned nothing. And, with the indifference of ignorance, he had left his brick in the galley—the fatal spot where it ought not to have been, in view of what was to happen.

For three stormy days the ship had been charging along before a wind that had increased to a gale, and a following sea that threatened to climb aboard. The jib-topsail, the skysails and royals, the lighter middle staysails, and the fore and mizzen topgallantsails had been blown away, and the ship was practically under topsails, a bad equipment of canvas with which to claw off a lee shore. The lee shore developed at daylight of the fourth stormy morning, a dim blue heightening of the horizon to the east, dead ahead; and Captain Williams, who had been unable to get a sight with his sextant for six days, could only determine that his dead reckoning, based upon the wild steering of his crew, had brought him too far to the north, and that the land he saw was the coast above Mizen Head.

After breakfast, when factory hours began, he called all hands to the braces; and they came, bracing the yards for the starboard tack, to keep away from that menacing lee shore; but, during the work, Murphy, by way of encouragement, called the crew's attention to the dim blot of blue to leeward.

"The Imerald Isle, boys," he declared. "Wark, ye watchmakers, wark, and git home."

They worked nobly, but wondered why the ship was heading away from the Emerald Isle, and expressed their wonder loudly and profanely. In vain did Murphy explain that Queenstown was around the corner to the south, and it was to Queenstown that they were bound. Their dissatisfaction grew, and at dinner-time lifted them above the weakening influence of the "sign language."

They had never taken account of the days when meat was due, ascribing the fixed hiatuses to the unkindness of the Chinese cook; and when they mustered at the galley door at noon and the cook handed them a huge pan of bean soup they raged at him, incoherently, but vehemently.

"Whaur's th' mate—the mate? Giv's the mate, ye haythen! giv's the mate, domyersool!"

The cook shrank back before their gleaming eyes and threatening fists, and they crowded into the galley, where, as fate determined, the mild little steward was gathering up the cabin dinner. He seized his brick.

"Now, here, you men," he said, bravely, "you get right out of this galley. Do you hear?" And he waved his brick threateningly.

"Whaur's the mate? Giv's the mate, ye man-killers."

"The mate is aft. You know that well as I do. Go right out of this galley."

"Whaur's the mate?"

"Aft in the cabin, I told you. Get out of here."

Even now things might have been well, for a few of them showed a willingness to go aft for the "mate." But the men of the other county came to the other galley door, and, menaced from both sides, the steward unwisely threw his brick. It struck the head of the foremost Irishman (it was the man on his wedding trip) and almost knocked him down. The cook frantically followed suit, and carnage began. The two gangs crowded into the narrow apartment, and the cook and steward soon went underfoot before the shower of fist-blows and kicks. They would assuredly have been injured in the *mêlée* had not a Limerick face approached too temptingly close to a Galway fist and diverted the storm. In utter fear of death the two crawled to the stove and pried up a couple of bricks while the rival factions fought each other. But their action was observed, and with whoops and oaths the combatants armed themselves, while the cook and steward crawled under the galley table for safety.

The captain and first mate were in the cabin, waiting for their dinner. The second mate was near the wheel, admonishing the Irish helmsman, as he dared, in the way of better steering "by-the-wind." Hennesey was in the port forecastle, just turning out after his forenoon watch below, and Murphy was amidships; but the sound of oaths, shrieks of rage and pain, and the incessant hammering of bricks upon the bulkheads and the pots and pans of the galley brought all to the scene, the captain and mates with their pistols.

"Hold on, Captain," said Murphy; "don't shoot any wan. Just let 'em fight it out, then they'll be more tractable."

This seemed reasonable, and the group watched from the main-hatch. There was a steady flight of bricks out through each galley door, some impacting upon the rails and falling to the deck, others going overboard. Occasionally an Irishman would reel out in company with the brick that had impelled him; but, after crawling around on all-fours for a moment, he would go back with a brick gleaned from the deck. At last, however, one came out with a little more momentum than usual—enough to carry him over to the rail; and from this point of view he could see the group at the hatch. He glared at them from under his tousled hair, then uttered a war-whoop.

"Ei-hei-ee, in thaur!" he yelled, "quit yer foolin' an' c'm'an out. Here be the bloody murders, the man-killers, the domned sons uv a landlord. C'm'an out, ye divils."

They heard, and they came, from both doors, with bloody faces and blackened eyes, and, seeing the captain and his aids, charged as one man. In vain Murphy's poised brick and Hennesey's persuasive voice. In vain the leveled pistols of the captain and mates and their thundering orders to stop or be shot down. There came a volley of bricks, and the captain's pistol was knocked from his hand, while a second brick, striking him on the head, robbed him of sense and volition. Each of the mates fired his pistol once, but not again; the bullets flew wide, and the firearms were twisted from their hands, while they were tripped up, struck, and kicked about until helpless to rise or resist. Hennesey and Murphy were also borne to the deck and punished. Some might have been killed had not one inspired Celt given voice to an original idea.

"Lock 'em up!" he shouted. "Lock 'em up in the kitchen, an' nail the dures on thim!"

They joyously accepted the suggestion. The four weak and stricken conscious men were dragged or shoved into the galley by some, while others lifted the unconscious captain after them. Then the doors were closed, and soon they heard the hammering of nails over the jangle of voices. Then the jangle of voices took on a new and distinct note of unanimity.

"Turn the boat, Denny," they shouted to the man at the wheel. "Turn the boat around. We'll go home in sphite o' thim, the vilyuns."

Their footfalls sounded fainter and fainter as they rushed aft; and Murphy picked himself up from the floor, now almost denuded of its brick paving.

"For the love of Gawd," he groaned, wiping the blood from his eyes, "are they goin' to beach her in this gale?"

The galley was lighted by two large deadlights, one each side, too small to crawl through, but large enough for a man's head. Murphy reached his head through one of them and looked aft. They had surrounded the wheel, and their war-cries were audible. As many as six were handling the spokes, and the big ship was squaring away before the wind, heading for that dim spot of blue in the murk and smoke to leeward. Murphy could see it when the ship pitched into a hollow— about forty miles away.

"And us locked up like rats in a trap," he muttered. "She'll strike in four hours, and Gawd help us all if we can't git out of here."

But there was no getting out, and they made the best of it. The cook and steward emerged from beneath the table, and made more or less frivolous comments on the condition of the galley and the ruin of the dinner, until silenced by the irate Murphy. The two mates took their hands from their aching heads and showed interest in life; and in time Captain Williams came to his senses and sat up on the floor, smeared with bean soup and cluttered with dented pots, pans, and stove-fittings. He was told the situation, and wisely accepted it; for nothing could be done.

And from aft came to their ears the joyous whoops of the homeward-bound men, close to their native land and anxious to get to it by the shortest route. Murphy occasionally looked out at them; they were all near the wheel, cursing and berating those handling the spokes, and being cursed in return. But they were not quarreling.

"Me brother Mike was right," muttered Murphy, as he drew his head in after a look at them. "They've forgotten their dinner. They'd rather fight than ate, but rather wark than fight."

The big, light ship, even with upper canvas gone and the yards braced to port, was skimming along over the heaving seas at a ten-knot rate, and Murphy's occasional glimpses of that growing landfall showed him details of rock and wood and red sandy soil that bespoke a steep beach and a rocky bottom. The air was full of spume and the gale whistled dismally through the rigging with a sound very much like that of Murphy's big base-burner in his Front Street boarding-house, when the chill wintry winds whistled over the housetops. He wondered if he would ever return.

"God help us, Skipper," he said, solemnly, "if we don't strike at high tide. For at low tide we'll go to pieces an' be drowned as the water rises."

"I looked it up this morning," said the captain, painfully; for he was still dazed from the effects of the brick. "It is high tide on this coast at four this afternoon."

"All to the good, as far as our lives are consarned," said Murphy; "and mebbe for your ship, Skipper. It'll be hard to salve her, of course; but she won't git the poundin' she'd get at low-water mark."

"I don't care. It's a matter for the underwriters. Don't bother me. I may kill you, Murphy, and your man Hennesey, some day, but not now. I'm too sick."

They waited in silence until the crash came—a sickening sound of riven timbers and snapping wire rope. Then, from the sudden stopping of the ship, there came a heightening and a strengthening of the song of the wind in the rigging, and the thumping of upper spars, jolted clear of their fastenings by the shock. Looking out, Murphy saw that the topgallantmasts, with their yards, were hanging by their gear, threatening to fall at any heave of the ship on her rocky bed. And he saw that the beach was not a hundred yards distant. Also, that the crew was flocking forward.

"Let us out of here," he called, as they came within hearing. "What more do ye want, ye bogtrotters? Ye've wrecked the man's boat, but d'ye want to kill us?"

"Yis," they chorused. "Why not, ye divils? Ye've nearly killed us all, dom yez. No mate, no whusky, no money. Tell us the road to Galway."

"An' the road to Limerick," said another. "An' whin do we git paid aff?"

"I'll have ye in jail, ye hyeenas," said Murphy. "That's yer pay, and that's the road to Galway and Limerick. Wait till the coast guard comes along. They'll git ye."

He drew back to avoid a brick that threatened to enter the deadlight, and the conversation ended.

Meanwhile the ship was slowly swinging around broadside to the beach. She was too high out of water for the seas to board her, though they pounded her weather side with deafening noise, and with each impact she was lifted shoreward a few feet more. Finally the crashings ceased, and they knew that, with water in the hold, she had gone as high as the seas could drive her. Then, with the going down of the tide, the heavy poundings of the sea grew less and the voices of the crew on the forecastle deck more audible.

"Can we make it in three jumps, Terrence?" they heard.

"No, ye fule. The wather's goin' down. Howld yer whist."

Murphy, looking out through the deadlight, could see nothing of the water between the ship and the beach; but far down to the south he discerned a team of horses dragging a wagon holding a boat, and this he explained to the skipper.

"The coast guard," explained the latter. "God grant that they get here before that bunch gets away. English law is severe upon mutineers."

But in this Captain Williams was doomed to disappointment. The coast guard arrived in time and released them. But before this each man of the twenty-four had passed before the open deadlight, derided and jeered the unlucky prisoners, called them unprintable names, and slid down the side on a rope to dry land.

Murphy looked at them climbing the hills inland, their whoops and yells coming back to him like pæans of victory.

"And what county do ye think this is, Skipper?" he asked.

"The county of Cork, of course," answered the captain.

"Well," said Murphy, "an enemy's country. We'll hope that the county o' Cork 'll take care o' thim. They're beyand you and me and Hennesey, Skipper."

Extracts from Noah's Log

While exploring the rocky gullies and canyons in the foothills of Mount Ararat last summer, I found a roughly symmetrical mass of pure copper. Oxidized and honeycombed as it was, I recognized the metal immediately, and repressing a strong inclination to hunt for the lead and stake out my claim, I took my find home with me. Surprised at its diminishing weight as the moisture dried out of the spongy mass, I endeavored to saw into it. The pure metal inside tore off every tooth of the saw, and now convinced that it was a hollow cylinder of hardened copper, I brought it to America and gave it to a machinist to open. He ruined two dozen finely-tempered saws in the job, which I cheerfully settled for, as the cylinder contained a papyrus roll of manuscript of certainly great antiquity.

My efforts to decipher it were baffled, as it was written in neither ancient nor modern Egyptian, new nor old Pali, nor in Greek, Latin, Sanscrit, nor in any other language with which I am acquainted. So I called in the services of two reverend friends of mine—able, eminent, and renowned professors of biology, bibliology, ethnology, and sockdology—who at once pronounced it ancient Cush and proceeded to translate it; one remarking with a levity which but indifferently became his calling, as I thought, that the exceeding toughness of the yarn no doubt accounted for the difficulty of sawing into it—in which view his collaborator, to my surprise, was inclined to coincide.

However, I cheerfully give them credit for the translation, but am free to maintain that the elegance of diction, force of expression, and choiceness of synonyms are my own.

Besides, I found it.

The Log

Mon., 7 days out. Raining yet, very hard—A few sinners still on deck; a bunch got washed off last night; kinder sorry for them—Ham will get a rope's-end if he don't look out; he skylarks too much with the animals; put all the dogs in the cats' cage last night, and the whole menagerie got excited at the row they made; couldn't hear ourselves think for two hours; every brute in the outfit sung his song—Roof leaks—Women say it's washday and have started in on the week's wash; just like women; how'll they dry clothes this weather?

Course E. B. S. Ham at the wheel, Shem on the lookout.

Tues., 8 days out. 4 bells. Women are growling because the sun don't shine so the wash can dry; told them such murmuring as they indulged in was flying straight in the face of Providence; told me to mind my own business; remarked that I was captain here and wouldn't take back talk from anyone; hove a bucket of water over me, durn them. *6 bells.* Got my log line strung up along 'tween decks and the whole blamed wash triced up in everybody's way. If I want to heave the log at 8 bells, overboard goes the wash, and don't care who likes it; I'm boss here. *8 bells.* Didn't heave the log—Guess we're making four knots; wind fresh.

Course E. S. E. Shem at the wheel, Japheth on the lookout.

Wed., 9 days out. Ironing day; blowing a gale of wind; women are making hard work of it and getting seasick—Hove to at 8 bells this morning; lays easy; kicked Ham away from the wheel and steered his trick; afraid I can't make a sailor of him; wish I'd saved a few sinners to work ship; could have drowned them afterwards.

Heading N. E. by N. Japheth at the wheel.

Thurs., 10 days out. Wish I knew who drinks my whiskey— Made sail at daylight; difficult work, this handling sail below decks; can't see aloft, must feel when sheets are home; don't like these new fangled rolling topsails that furl themselves; they're not shipshape, but we're too short-handed for the old style—Wind going down.

Course due E. Shem at the wheel, Ham on the lookout.

Fri., 11 days out. Foggy; can't see two lengths; two of us on the lookout—Ham is under the scuttlebutt, drunk; whiskey lower; slight connection here, maybe—Women are quarreling among themselves; they're a heap of trouble; never quiet till they're seasick; found out they get seasick in a head sea; will remember this—The lion got out last night and made a lunch out of my wife's pet dog Beauty; chased him back to his cage with a handspike; sorry I had to hurt him; seven pugs left now; we started with a pair to each woman.

No wind and nobody at the wheel.

Sat., 12 days out. Wish it would clear up; sinners must be all dead by this time—Have had a hard day of it; that boy Ham let go the port anchor, and the whole range of chain, 45 fathoms, went out the hawse-pipe and fetched up with a jerk that carried away the windlass bitts and nearly tore the bows off her; kicked him up on deck in the rain while we mended the windlass; hunted him up to help heave in chain and found he'd sneaked down, got at my jug, and was dead drunk alongside the same; don't see what the Lord wanted to save him for—Must be clear of soundings now, so will keep her hove to for a while under short sail, with the wheel lashed down.

Sun., 13 days out. Held religious exercises at 4 bells; Ham attended, very devout and penitent, with a head as big as the jug—Women have tricked themselves out and are mincing around showing off; made me put on a white shirt; will get rid of it directly—Dead calm all day—Found the ark had a slight list to starboard; investigated, and discovered about three tons of stones, dead cats, and garbage stuck fast to the pitch outside; these things are what the sinners threw at the ark after we came aboard—Have locked up my whiskey.

Wed., 16 days out. Made a great mistake when we started; was puzzled how to feed the spiders, mosquitoes, bedbugs, and such; turned them loose to hustle for themselves, and that's what they've done ever since—Another pug disappeared last night; six left; gave Ham a talking to about getting drunk; was sassy and I boxed his ears; told him if I ever saw him drunk again aboard my ship I'd log him; he don't seem to care, but that's what I'll do every time—Still hove to.

Sun., 20 days out. Ham broke into my locker last night, and is roaring drunk again; can't find the jug; will log him every time now—No religious exercises to-day; women are complaining of my impiety, but a man can't feel resigned when he has just lost a four-gallon jug of the best Egyptian corn whiskey.

Mon., 21 days out. Ham's drunk.

Tues., 22 days out. Ditto's ditto.

Wed., 23 days out. Do. do.

Thurs., 24 days out. Do. blind do.

Fri., 25 days out. Do. dead do.

Sat., 26 days out. Do. got snakes; got 'em bad; wish I could find that jug.

Sun., 27 days out. Two more pugs missing; must keep away from the lion's cage when the women are around; he seems too pleased to see me, and they are getting suspicious; four of the ugly brutes left now—found my jug; Ham stowed it in my own bunk; he's smarter than I thought—Had religious exercises; women wanted to mourn for their pugs; am willing they should mourn—Took a cast of the lead at noon; thirty fathoms, mud bottom; made sail and squared away due E.

Mon., 28 days out. My wife has confiscated the jug and means to keep it; we'll see about that; says it is the cause of poor, dear Ham's sickness; undoubtedly; should have let it alone— Shem at the wheel, Japheth on the lookout.

Course E.

Wed., 30 days out. Mutiny! Bloody Mut— d—n! —!!
(Note—Here the manuscript bears evidence that Captain
Noah was suddenly interrupted while writing.—Translator.)

Fri., 32 days out. Have had a lively time; discipline is restored,
but the whiskey jug is gone—smashed over my head—all
on account of the pugs; had hoped to rid the world of these
parodies on the canine race, and would have succeeded if my
wife hadn't overhauled my pockets when I was asleep and
read this log. Certain references to the pugs put her on the
lookout and she and the other women watched me; one of
the brutes littered that night; I couldn't resist the temptation,
and so fed the whole batch, mother and all, to the lion; in
a minute had four furious women afoul of me, biting and
clawing; sung out for help, and Shem and Japheth bore
down and rescued me; Ham helped the women and made
a majority for them; his mother had the jug, that's why;
managed to floor him with a pump-brake, but they were
still too many for us and chased us around decks till they got
tired and sat down to cry; got to my room and began writing
them down in the log when they started in again; my wife
smashed the whiskey jug over my head—then we all escaped
on deck and went aloft; couldn't follow us, but sat down
and said things—Had a council of war, then Shem shinned
over to the foremast and cut away all the jib halliards and
sheets and halliards on the fore—Ark had broached to in
trough sea when Japheth left the wheel to help me, and
had laid there with yards square and rolling considerable;
women could stand that motion, but not a head sea, so
now when she came up to the wind and began pounding
up and down and drifting astern, they got qualmish and
in twenty minutes were sprawled out helpless; Ham didn't
know enough to take the wheel and throw her off, so we
came down, tied the women hand and foot, and then went
for Ham; triced him up and rope's-ended him till his nose
bled; begged and howled, but had to take it and learn that
mutiny is unsafe aboard my ship—Kept her head to the sea
till we had spliced and rove off the gear, then set canvas and
squared away again—Women got better; read the articles

to them; were penitent and promised to behave, but before turning them loose we went on a pug hunt and passed two of them in to the lion; only one left now, but we haven't found it yet; women howled a good deal and called us heartless, cruel fiends—that's all right.

My wife had lost the log-book in her excitement, and I only found it to-day.

Course N. E. by E. Shem at the wheel. Jap. on the lookout.

Sun., 34 days out. No religious services to-day; women are talking about me—don't talk *to* me; if they do, I'll speak of that jug.

Course due E. Blowing fresh. J. at the wheel, S. on lookout.

Mon., 35 days out. Wash day, but there is no washing going on; won't have it; am captain here; they were ugly at first, but I hauled her on a wind and said nothing; can't find that pug—Keep Ham at work on the menagerie now, feeding the animals and cleaning the cages—Dead calm.

Wed., 37 days out. Nothing new; pug still missing; good mind to turn the lion loose; he'll find the cur.

Fri., 39 days out. If I don't find that pug to-day, will let the lion out first thing to-morrow.

Sat., 40 days out. Stopped raining—We all went on deck this morning; it was a frightful picture—sun shining, not a cloud in the sky and not a sign of land nor ship, nor even a bird, in all this expanse of desolation; no life nor joyousness, nothing but muddy water; the dead world fathoms underneath, and we alone, with our ark, all that was left; and whiskey gone—not a shot in the locker.

At noon locked up the women and turned the lion loose; he didn't find the pug, but found most everything else; smashed some bird cages and a raven and dove got away; dove came back at sundown, but the raven didn't; let all the birds out to get the air and roost up aloft.

Sat., 47 days out. Chicken missing this morning; suspect Ham of stealing it—A pigeon fluttered down on deck with a green leaf fast in its gullet and half choked; pulled leaf out; pigeon must have been somewhere else and got it; will keep to the eastward and look out for land.

Tues., 50 days out. Blowing great guns, and dismasted; under double reefs, storm spanker, and foretopmast staysail at daylight; blew away the staysail; set jib; that went too and took jibboom; cut away the wreck; she came up to the wind, caught aback, and away went the mizzenmast at the deck; cut that away, paid off in the trough of the sea, and rolled the fore and mainmast out; cleared away everything, rigged out a sea anchor, and now were riding it out comfortable—that is, for us; women are all sick.

Land to the eastward, small island.

60 days out. Land still in sight; gets bigger; suppose the water is going down; nothing to do now but eat, sleep, and hunt for that pug—Still riding at the sea anchor.

100 days out. Pug must be dead—More land showing up.

150 days out. Noon—Driving on a lee shore stern foremost; getting anchors ready; *sundown*—let go both anchors as we got close in; dragged, and here we are, with every sea making a clean sweep over us; ark won't last long; getting out liferaft and turning animals loose.

Next morning. Floated ashore all right; ark is breaking up and animals swimming in; last to come were that missing pug and seven half-grown pups; submit to the will of Providence, but still think women had the durned brute hid in the lower hold.

Next day. Poor place to live on this island—Nothing grown, but a grapevine I found on the beach; will take care of it; it means grapes, and grapes mean juice, and it's been a long time between drinks—Ham is quite useful now; takes a deep interest in the vine and helps me 'tend it.

Month later. Grapevine is doing well.

Four months later. Grapes appearing.

Two months later. Picked the grapes; now for some wine— Ham is a model boy; did him good to rope's-end him.

Five months later. Wine has worked; will serve grog to-morrow and celebrate the anniversary of our shipwreck.

Next day. (The manuscript of this last day's entry is obscure, and so incoherent, as to make it strongly probable that Captain Noah served the grog as indicated, and that he wrote while under the influence of the same. There are, however, some legible references to certain "pugs" which would go to show that he still had those animals in mind and perhaps regretted his failure to effect their extinction.)

A Note About the Author

Morgan Robertson (1861–1915) was an American novelist and short story writer. Born into a seafaring family, Robertson entered the merchant service as a teenager, rising to the rank of first mate by the time of his departure in 1886. With his sailing days behind him, Robertson studied jewelry making and worked in New York City as a diamond setter for 10 years. During this time, he also wrote sea stories and novels, including *Futility, or the Wreck of the Titan* (1898), a novel with a striking similarity to the sinking of the Titanic in 1912. Despite seeing his work published in *McClure's* and the *Saturday Evening Post*, Robertson failed to make a living as a professional writer, leading to a deep dissatisfaction also fueled by the author's claims to have not received credit for his invention of the submarine periscope. Despite his lack of popular success and critical acclaim, Robertson's work is thought to have influenced such writers as Edgar Rice Burroughs and Henry De Vere Stacpoole.

A Note from the Publisher

bookfinity™

Discover more of your favorite classics with Bookfinity™.

- Track your reading with custom book lists.
- Get great book recommendations for your personalized Reader Type.
- Add reviews for your favorite books.
- AND MUCH MORE!

Visit **bookfinity.com** and take the fun Reader Type quiz to get started.

Enjoy our classic and modern companion pairings!

Classic & Modern

Printed in the USA
CPSIA information can be obtained
at www.ICGtesting.com
JSHW082350140824
68134JS00020B/2002

9 781513 281490